The Death of the Perfect Sentence

Rein Raud

translated by
Matthew Hyde

Vagabond Voices
Glasgow

First published in June 2017 by
Vagabond Voices Publishing Ltd.,
Glasgow,
Scotland.

ISBN 978-1-908251-70-1

Printed and bound in Poland

Cover design by Mark Mechan

Typeset by Park Productions

The publisher acknowledges subsidy
towards this translation from the
Estonian Cultural Endowment

EESTI KULTUURKAPITAL

The publisher acknowledges subsidy towards
this publication from Creative Scotland

ALBA | CHRUTHACHAIL

For further information on Vagabond Voices, see the website,
www.vagabondvoices.co.uk

The Death of the
Perfect Sentence

I am aware that the following story contains departures from the historical truth. The spot where pickets were held from spring to autumn was not in fact visible from the café where the two men were sitting. The statue of Kalevipoeg referred to does not exist, nor did the sculptor who might have created it. And even if it had stood where I put it, I doubt that it could have been used in the way described. And so forth. Memory is unreliable. Time speeds up. Successive summers merge into one. I can only apologise.

As is written in the classics, any similarities with real events are coincidental, but all names have been left unchanged.

There are two of them, sitting on the café terrace, at the far end by the railing, from where there is a good view of the square, and one of them is holding a pair of binoculars for that very purpose. They could be brothers judging by the similarity of their faces, which are expressionless and unre-markable. On closer inspection, it's difficult to say exactly what makes them seem alike. They are both wearing exactly the same type of suit: dark, poorly fitting, evidently stand-ard issue. Totally unsuitable for today's warm weather. And they both have the same kind of glass on the table in front of them, one-third full of mineral water.

There is no one else there. It's quiet, apart from the barely audible murmur of the street. Earlier there was a group of young punks as well, but as soon as the two men arrived, the scruffy lads' and the blue-haired girls' beer-addled banter turned into an agitated whisper, and they got up, paid their bill, and left. From then on the two men had the whole place to themselves.

They don't exchange a single word. They just sit there looking over the railing, towards the square. Not that it looks in any way different from yesterday, the day before yesterday, or the day before that. Worried, weary people walking past avoiding each other's gazes, the occasional tourist wandering around distractedly, a Communist Party slogan hanging on the wall of the grey building, and outside it the same pickets who have already been there for several weeks, holding banners demanding "Occupying forces out of Estonia!" and "Release Aare Murakas!" You can show your support for the latter with a signature. Some people do. There is a large glass jar for you to donate your rapidly depreciating roubles in support of the struggle for freedom. Some do that too, and the jar is already half full. Friends and strangers come up and shake hands, others wave from a distance. Some of them chuckling, some wary, others looking around with frightened expressions on their faces. In case anyone spots them there.

Those two men are not in the slightest bit interested in who Aare Murakas is or what he may or may not think about things, nor do they consider the forces whose withdrawal is called for to be occupation forces. But neither are they particularly worried about the pickets. Not just because they don't take the whole independence movement very seriously. It's just a bunch of kids after all. Has a mosquito ever floored an elephant? These two men have never read the Bible, and for them David and Goliath is just a Jewish legend with no bearing on reality. Something is about to happen here nevertheless. That is why they're sitting on this café terrace right now.

A young man and woman walk up to the café and have already started to sit down when they notice the two men. The young man says a couple of words, out of earshot, to the woman, then they both stand up and hurriedly leave.

The pickets' faces are clearly visible through the binoculars. They are recognisable from the intelligence files, especially Ervin, a lanky young man with curly red hair and freckles, who is the reason they are there. Ervin is edgy. His companions have no idea why. They probably don't even notice that he is hopping from foot to foot, as if he needs the toilet. Perhaps he really does. But even if he doesn't, Ervin is known to be the restless type. The two men know what the problem really is: Ervin has made his choice. It's not surprising that a person who is about to do something life-changing is a little edgy. Because Ervin is the only one who knows the two men are there. He also knows that one or the other of them is watching him constantly waiting for him to give the sign. That's why he's so edgy. And he can't even think about going to the toilet until he has done what he has to do.

By now the waitress is fed up with these two men. The mineral water in their glasses has not gone down; a normal customer would have downed two beers in the length of time they've been there. This is a café, after all. People come here to eat and drink. There are other places to sit and birdwatch. The waitress is fully prepared to point all this out to them. Expressionless faces and out-of-place dark suits clearly don't confer any special privileges. She approaches their table and opens her mouth to speak. That's when she notices the bulges in their breast pockets and the bulky walkie-talkie on one of their knees. And so she says, "Would you like anything else?"

"No thank you," one of them replies.

Indrek walked slowly past the Kiek in de Kök tower and along the tarmac road which led down one side of Harjumäe Park. Almost no one apart from the odd map buff and a couple of city government staff knew that its official name was Soviet Street. Indrek was in a good mood, and he had some time on his hands, even if he now only had a couple of ten-rouble notes left in the wallet in the pocket of his construction brigade jacket, and they had to last him for a while yet. As far as his parents knew he was still working with that construction brigade, building some stupid barn at a collective farm out in some stupid backwater. In the old days they used to pay you properly for that kind of work. Now you got peanuts. It may have seemed a large sum of money in spring when the wages were agreed, but by the time it reached Indrek's wallet, if it actually got there, it wouldn't buy him much. And there was just so much happening across the country. In Indrek's view the kind of people who were happy to build some stupid barn out in some stupid backwater while history passed them by or ran roughshod over them fully deserved their fate. That wasn't for him. He'd reached the age of majority, having turned eighteen two months ago, and now he was allowed to drive a car, get married, vote and be elected. He was ready to make his own choices. Living at his father's house in Keila was no longer one of them. So he'd been in Tallinn for three weeks now, staying here and there with different friends, his hand firmly on the pulse of history. It was beating in different places, in different ways, but he wasn't too bothered about all the friction between the political forces. That was just a surface tremor, they were all working to a common goal.

And while all that was going on Indrek was also busy trying to find himself a soulmate. When a whiff of freedom is in the air, people open up too, and start seeing endless open avenues all around them. Or at least that was what he hoped.

5

Indrek was a spotty-faced youngster who read a lot, and he'd chipped teeth too. Sometimes he managed to meet a girl who didn't need to be told who the Strugatskys or Bradbury or Lem or Simak were, and everything would go quite well. That is until he tried to put his arms around her and bring his face close to hers. Then he would discover, much to his surprise, that their earlier bond was broken, or completely lost, even if they could carry on talking about the same things almost as before. When he later saw that same girl dancing with one of his friends, with her arms around him and her vision dimmed by a romantic mist, he felt completely crushed. Maybe his teeth were the problem. The dentist was to blame for the state they were in. During his school years, one dreaded day in the dismal depths of winter, the nurse would look round the classroom door and yell out the names of the pupils who had to see the dentist. They would come back clutching new dental records, and one by one the whole class would go. Two or three dentists set themselves up in the school nurse's office, where they checked every single pupil. Their equipment was old and basic, and the resulting pain was excruciating, but the dentists were in a hurry, they had several hundred children to get through. When the dentist first checked Indrek all she could do was let out a shriek. What horrible teeth! Naturally it meant a lot of tedious work, seeing that same spotty boy again and again, until she could put a tick in the box and place Indrek's dental records on the other pile. And she did all that with equipment which was even older and more worn out than she was. Of course Indrek looked forward to those appointments even less than the dentist. Once during Christmas his first two fillings fell out, leaving him facing the New Year in much the same situation as before. It didn't help matters that Indrek liked to suck sweets as he read; in fact he scoffed them and could polish off a whole bag of Goose Feet chews or Golden Key toffees without noticing. But one year things were different – Indrek somehow got hold of a book about scientists from the Loodus publisher's "Golden Book" series, published during the first Estonian Republic. There he learned that the inventor of the microscope, Antonie van Leeuwenhoek, never had a single problem with his teeth, because he rubbed them with a goose feather every day after brushing, just as his mother had taught him. Indrek couldn't lay his hands on a goose feather, but he decided that a flannel would serve the same purpose, and this proved to be right – next autumn he found that for the first time he didn't have a single cavity. But having proven his hypothesis to himself, his perseverance did not last. By the time he finished middle school his parents were forced to completely replace his rotten front teeth. What happened to the rest of his teeth was going to be his own business.

Why am I talking about Indrek's teeth at such length? Don't ask.

Indrek walked down Toompea and thought about turning off to sit outside the café for a while, since spring had at last fully broken out and it was the time of day when you could find company there. But today it was quiet at the café. Just two men sitting there, looking out of place in black suits, one of them observing someone or something on the other side of the square through binoculars. Indrek suddenly stopped, and the realisation of what this meant came to him in a moment, faster than lightning, like an electric shock. He'd previously had a vague awareness of it, but then it existed only theoretically, in books, or somewhere deeper down, in the horror stories which the other boys had tormented him with at night when he and his elder brother were first sent to Pioneer camp for summer. Now, however, that abstract evil had begun to spread its poison; that blackest of cats was right there in front of him, it had stepped across the threshold and into his life. What else could those two men have been put there for?

He faltered for a moment and then, as if on a whim,

turned off the road and descended the steps to the square, stopping when he reached the theatre posters. There was no way those two men could have noticed him slowing down momentarily, but he could still sense their presence behind him.

His friends were standing there in the picket and evidently didn't suspect a thing.

As Karl walked across the bumpy paving towards the grey building his heart was racing. It would continue to do so for the next half an hour. Today certainly wasn't the first time he'd put himself in danger, and it felt the same as it always did. It was necessary for freedom, for all of us. But the panic pulsating in his ears as he moved his arms and legs through sheer force of will – that was entirely for him to deal with.

He spotted the pickets from some way off and decided to wait at a safe distance, hoping that one of his friends would notice him. Who knows, someone might still be watching the picket from a distance, even if the authorities had apparently got used to it by now. Evidently it had been decided somewhere high up that dispersing the picket would do more harm than letting it be. But he still didn't want to provoke any trouble. He noticed one of the guys approaching – they were all younger than him: his own university days were behind him and he'd already endured two years of pointless, mind-numbing work. The youth was short, with thick-rimmed glasses, a sports bag slung over his shoulder; he looked like he could still be at school. Nothing other than the struggle for freedom had any meaning for the likes of him. Karl liked to think that these guys could learn a thing or two from him. He would have been surprised to find out what they really thought of him – after all he didn't smoke and wasn't into sport. And he was always so smartly dressed. He obviously took trouble over his appearance: his shirts were ironed, trousers pressed, shoes polished. A presentable exterior was a prerequisite for internal order; clear thinking required cleanliness. But he didn't know what he looked like to others: always pale and feverish, black hair dishevelled, constantly in danger of having a nosebleed.

This guy must have been new, because Karl didn't know his name. He beckoned Karl to one side, a couple of steps under the arch, and took a fatter than usual envelope from his bag.

"Where did you get to?" he asked. "We have to hurry now."

"I know," said Karl with a nod. "I couldn't get away from work any earlier."

"Fair enough," the lad said, and he darted off back on to the street without saying goodbye. A moment later he was back standing where he'd been before, leaving Karl in the courtyard counting to fifty.

What was inside the envelope

Neither Karl nor the young man (his name was Anton) knew what was in the envelope, nor could they have done. In the interests of clarity it shall be revealed that it contained a videotape (Video-8 format, cutting-edge technology at the time) and a dozen photographs of Soviet soldiers using sharpened sappers' shovels to beat peaceful demonstrators who had assembled in Rustaveli Avenue in central Tbilisi to protest against Abkhazia's secession bid from Georgia. Nineteen people died as a result, including seventeen women. It was clear from the pictures that the soldiers had initiated the violence and were taking advantage of the opportunity to attack defenceless protestors, rather than protecting themselves against an aggressive crowd, as the official version had claimed. That was what was inside the fatter-than-usual envelope.

Karl made sure not to look at the pickets as he walked past them, just as he'd been taught. But that didn't help.

He still had to walk through the line of sight of the binoculars, which were pointed from the direction of the café.

He didn't notice the particular way in which Ervin ran his hand through his curly red hair at that very moment, but the two men sitting outside the café certainly did.

What? An envelope which was fatter than usual.

Where to? A certain tree hollow.

The less time these two pieces of information were known to the same person the better.

All that time Indrek had been leaning against the wall, lost in thought, unable to fully understand what was going on or how he should act. Or to be more precise: he suspected that what was happening was one of those occasional historical turbulences which could end up dragging down anyone who got too close, engulfing them in an indiscriminate torrent of events. Indrek had no intention of letting that happen to him. But nor could he just stand back and watch. He had no time to warn Karl about what was happening. He didn't actually see the envelope being handed over, but he certainly sensed that something significant was taking place right there and then. He was also aware that the two men had got up and left the café. A moment later they were already walking past him, and as in a dream he found himself unable to resist following them. They didn't notice him – just as the adder slithering after the field mouse often doesn't notice the eagle circling above. Indrek glanced back over his shoulder now and again so as to avoid making the same mistake himself.

Karl was also looking about edgily, but he couldn't see the people who were following him. They'd parted company: one was holding back a little distance from Karl, who had made his way round the back of the Estonia Theatre and was hurrying through Tammsaare Park, while the other was following at a steady pace roughly twenty metres back. Indrek had his work cut out just to keep up with them. In his haste he nearly tripped over a little boy who despite the warm weather was wrapped up in winter clothes and tottering about helplessly amongst the pigeons. Indrek had no choice but to stop and listen as the boy's grandmother, who was dressed in a brown felt coat and lilac headscarf, explained to him in a shrill voice how he was supposed to walk in the park. Indrek apologised as politely as he knew how, looking about the whole time. For a moment it seemed he'd lost sight of Karl and the spooks who were tailing him, but it was just that the two men had swapped places. One of them had come to a standstill, and by the time Indrek passed him, just before reaching the Kaubamaja department store, the man had slipped under an archway and was speaking on his walkie-talkie. Fortunately he was standing with his back to the street. There were more people here, so dodging through the crowd attracted more attention, but the spooks were so sure of themselves that they suspected nothing.

Karl had been informed about the location that morning, on a card pushed through his letterbox. It depicted Kreshchatyk Street in central Kiev, not St Basil's Cathedral in Red Square, nor the Hermitage in Leningrad. That meant that he had to stuff the envelope into a certain tree hollow in Pasatski park. Karl hadn't previously had to deliver anything in the daytime and in such a busy area, and his heart was pounding, but if that was the instruction, there must be a good reason for it. His heart pounding, he glanced around and put his briefcase down. A couple of benches ahead, a man with the typical purple nose was gripping a bottle of beer, but he seemed to be sufficiently occupied with his own personal problems. Karl removed the envelope from his briefcase and took a couple of steps on to the grass, in the direction of the right tree.

What happened next was like in a film. Probably. He didn't watch those kinds of films himself, because the role of the good guy was always given to the upstanding Soviet intelligence officers, whom he could not stand. Maybe what happened next was actually the reverse of those films, but that wasn't important. Two men dressed in identical ill-fitting suits appeared in the park as if from nowhere. Karl watched them like a rabbit hypnotised into submission by a cobra: he couldn't even move his arms, to say nothing of trying to run away. He watched with a frozen gaze, as if observing the scene from one remove, as the envelope was yanked from his hand, his arms were twisted behind his back, and he was marched back the way he'd come, towards the park entrance. But then he recalled that a few moments earlier his temporal lobe had registered the screech of brakes. An unmarked black Volga with two men in it, one driving and one in the front passenger seat, had driven on to the footpath. Just as he realised what was happening. He was bundled into the back of the car, and one of the men who had been following him got in, coming crashing down beside him.

The other man came to a standstill next to the car, opened the envelope, looked at the photos of the brutish soldiers beating the Georgian women with spades and shook his head.

"Fucking degenerates," he mumbled to himself. It went without saying that the rest of the world should never be allowed to see photographs like this.

He took his walkie-talkie out from inside his coat, stepped off the path and under the trees.

"All taken care of," he reported. "I'll stay here on guard."

A word about telephones.

I'm not sure where to start, or how to write about this without making it seem trivial. It's a question of *feelings* (most things are a question of feelings, let's not pretend otherwise). I was probably still in the last year of kindergarten when a telephone first appeared in our house – or maybe I'd already started the first year of school. Our telephone number was 442-75. Our first telephone was pretty ugly, and it was probably issued to us with the number, but soon it was replaced by a really cool red one which was to sit on father's big writing desk. At that time we lived in two rooms of a communal flat, together with two other families. Me and my brother Mihkel shared one room, and my parents were in the other one, where father also worked. The flat was in an old and soundly built pre-war building, with high ceilings and a spacious corridor. There was also a Pescadas toilet dating from the first Estonian Republic in the bathroom. I remember that there were also neatly cut squares of newspaper on the nail meant for toilet paper, and at one point there were Soviet state loan bonds there too, given to Soviet workers in the 1950s as part of their salary. By the time I started using that toilet the workers had long lost all hope of being able to cash in those bonds.

The red phone is my brother Mihkel's most enduring memory of that flat, but possibly he was as a child in awe of that intermittently clanging object, and our parents later told him that it was his main memory from the time. Who knows? Human memory is a wondrous thing.

Not that my brother and I had much need for a telephone when we lived in that apartment. It was in our new home on Harju Street, where we moved after my sister was born, that I soon developed an out-and-out addiction to it. I would sometimes talk to friends for hours on end. We didn't play battleships – at least not very often – but we talked at length about anything we could think of. In those days we didn't have to pay for phone calls, and I constantly kept the line engaged, which really annoyed our parents.

Two smells

I have said this before, and I will say it again: two smells are lost from my life, one of them was a good one, one of them bad, but both were my companions for a long time. How could I have forgotten them? When I woke, especially on Sunday mornings, they came to greet me through the open window: burning briquettes and freshly baked pastries. Our home had municipal heating, whereas black smoke billowed from the chimneys in the old town, dissolved into the air and mingled with the smell of pastries coming from the shops on Karja Street and the Pearl and Tallinn cafés. Within moments of waking I'd pulled on my trousers and shirt, done up my laces and was out the door! The pastries were still warm when they reached our breakfast table, and there was rarely anything left over: folded puff pastries and feather-light curd cheese pockets, but best of all, those Vienna pastries topped with yellow confectioner's cream, which the Communist Party and government had decreed should be called Moscow pastries, even if no one had ever heard of them in Moscow. Sometimes they arrived straight out of the oven, left to cool on the back table of the shop just long enough to be put in the bag. Meanwhile, deposits of briquette smoke built up on our windowpanes, and most probably in our lungs too — there is probably some left even now. Both of those smells disappeared at almost exactly the same time. The briquette smoke wafted away with the people who moved from the old town to the new city districts, making way for better-off occupants. New pipes, new cabling, and new heating were installed in those grimy old houses. And the pastry shops closed their doors for the last time, because those pastries were replaced with a product which always tasted exactly the same, made by people somewhere far away, whose names and faces we did not know.

When I was at university I used to go to a public telephone centre to call home, and I had to book a call in advance and wait for the line to become available. Sometimes that could take a whole hour. Later, public phones appeared and you could slide your fifteen-kopeck coins into the slot and make the call yourself, but that didn't speed things up much. After taking a while to dial the number, you would usually end up hearing the slow engaged tone coming from the handset at the end of its twisting metallic cord. But at least you felt you were in control; you dialled the number with your own fingers, without being at the whim of some old crone sitting behind the counter.

And so the feeling is very familiar to me. You need to tell someone something important – that you love them very much, for example – but they just aren't home. Fifteen minutes later they are still not there. And fifteen minutes after that.

Our mental landscape was entirely different back then. There were the connecting nodes and then there were big black holes, a wilderness where your cry would never be heard. It was impossible to phone someone directly: you could only phone one of these connecting points, without knowing whether or not the person would actually answer.

I remember an advert for mobile phones which covered the whole side of a Tallinn tram. I can't remember exactly what year it was, but it was some time immediately after independence, in the early 1990s. It was an advert for a really tiny handset, much more elegant than those you would normally see people with, with a price tag of twelve thousand kroons. My salary at the time was somewhere in the region of one thousand kroons a month, so this was more or less my income for a year (and we were relatively well off).

But that was all later, some time later than the day in question, when Indrek stood by the corner of the grey fire station and observed what was happening, and then hurried off to look for a public phone to call Raim, the person who had ended up in the role of leader of their small group, who was only called Raimond by his parents. In those days the main worries associated with telephones were whether you had a two-kopeck coin on you, whether the phone you found actually worked, and whether the person you called would be home. Not whether so-and-so's phone battery might be flat, or whether someone is inside the coverage area. Times change, but problems remain.

At the moment when the telephone rings, Raim is sitting having lunch with his parents. There is a tablecloth on the table, not because it is some sort of special occasion, but because that had always been the custom in Raim's mother's home, even if it meant they had to wash their tablecloths more often; they had a washing machine for that very purpose. Not one of those front-loading *Vyatka* automatics with a window in the door – she wasn't sure whether she could really trust one of those – but the far simpler *Aurika*, where you had to lift your washing from one compartment to another so that the drier could do its work. But anyway, Raim's mother has cooked some meatballs today. And at this very moment Raim's father has just lifted up a mouthful on the end of his fork, and it is halfway to his open mouth. We don't realise straightaway that they are meatballs, because they are swamped in sauce. Raim's mother is in the habit of simmering her meatballs in sauce for a few minutes before serving them, again because this was the custom in her family – even though Raim and his father preferred their meatballs dry and crunchy. But the piece of meat on the end of Raim's father's fork hasn't come to a standstill halfway to his mouth because he's fighting his aversion to the food. No, Raim's father's mouth is open because he's preparing to say something. And he knows exactly what that will be, even if he hasn't fully formulated the sentence yet. Clearly it will be something to do with politics. Raim's father wants to say that in the current situation only a crazy person, someone who is totally ignorant, who has taken complete leave of their senses, an idiot in fact, would say anything to rock the boat, which is sailing steadily towards a better and freer life. It's never a good idea to poke a sleeping bear. The finest minds in the West have said that too, experts in their field, Sovietologists in academic institutes, each with a budget bigger than the whole Estonian economy. Moscow holds the keys. It isn't a good idea to be hasty now that the straightjacket is starting to come apart at the seams. They should just keep moving cautiously towards the destination and be happy with what they have. For him personally it's more important that he can go on a trip to Finland without having to apply for permission from the relevant departments (and that he's allowed to exchange more than thirty-five roubles), not whether the blue, white and black flag of Estonian independence flutters on the Tall Hermann tower of Toompea Castle. And he's convinced that the majority of the Estonian people, or at least those who are capable of thinking rationally, are of exactly the same opinion. Raim's father knows that once he has formulated and stated his sentence it will lead to an argument. That Raimond, his only son, this blond-haired, broad-shouldered boy with his wilfully jutting chin, who can become all those things which he was not, will disagree with him again. That's how it normally goes. He doesn't like it, and who would, but he's resigned to it. At least that way he has some sort of relationship with his son. It was the same way with his own father when he was young. And so he is annoyed when the phone call interrupts his chain of thought. But Raim is not, because for him those arguments with his father have long since lost any purpose. He doesn't yet know who is calling, or if the call is even for him, but he has already decided that if someone is looking for him, then he will use it as an excuse to flee this scene of domestic bliss. So what if he is still hungry. If the meatballs weren't covered in sauce, he would pick one up as he ran out of the room. But this is the way things are.

Things weren't exactly how the authorities thought they were back then: that a multitude of isolated, downtrodden people were embracing a vision of happiness and a historical mission which required them to speak a foreign language and to celebrate a foreigner's victories – a vision which promised to unite them, to restore them, to make them greater. Neither were things as some people like to remember them today: cinders glowing valiantly in every hearth, ready to blaze up into a tall, proud flame as soon as the first bugle call was heard. There was a quiet war being waged for sure, but it was so quiet that even the sharpest ears might not pick up the rumble of its cannons, and the clever chaps abroad had concluded that peoples' backs were so bowed that they would never stand upright again. That is until the newspapers told them quite how wrong they had been, leaving them unable to explain exactly what had happened. There was a quiet war being fought, but without a frontline moving backwards and forwards on demarcated territory. In the place of trenches there was something more like the circulation of blood, or mushroom spores: thousands, hundreds of thousands of little frontlines, passing through meeting rooms, wedding parties, family photographs, through individual people, who could be upstanding Soviet functionaries from nine to five and then turn into fervent idealists watching Finnish television in the evenings. But there is no point in asking if things could have been otherwise, only why those people's descendants are the same to this day, even if they have changed their colours. The printed money wasn't worth much back then, even if there were plenty of sweaty-palmed people with no scruples about handling it. There was however another important currency in circulation – trust. Some may use simpler terms such as acquaintances, contacts, but nothing would have counted without trust. Because in the end it was impossible to trust anyone if you hadn't gone to school together, shared the same sauna, gone scrumping with them, studied together, worked in the same office, done military service together, stolen something, eaten and drunk with them, slept with them. If you trusted someone, you could share your books, your telephone numbers, your smoked sausage, your summer house, anything you had, even trust itself – names, places, times. You didn't use a dentist whom you didn't trust, you didn't ask someone to pass a letter to your Swedish relatives if you didn't trust them. If you could help it you had nothing to do with people you did not trust – they might very well be working for the other side.

Trust was the only valid currency.

It was just so exhausting.

And so we used that trust to pay for our freedom, and we're still collecting the change to this day.

If you happen to be a citizen of the Kingdom of Sweden, and your name is Kenneth Lindblom, then you can be quite sure that your decision to stay at Kungla Hotel instead of the more usual Viru Hotel would have led to questions in the relevant departments. So what if you also happen to be a television reporter and Kungla Hotel is across the road from the offices of Estonian Television. Viru Hotel is not more than a short walk from there either. But Kungla Hotel lacks all those things which you, as a citizen of Sweden, might expect from a visit to the Soviet Union (since you're not a pensioner, and a bus trip to the ruins of Pirita Cloister or a visit to the building complex which hosted the 1980 Olympic regatta are probably of no interest to you). In Kungla Hotel there is no hard currency bar with its lavish selection of drinks; there is not even a hard currency shop where you can buy yourself a six-pack of Finnish beer to quaff in the quiet of your room. And the room itself leaves a lot to be desired. But above all there are no hard-currency prostitutes with respectable exteriors and perfectly tolerable Finnish but smiles which instantly give them away. Of course the relevant departments know that you are a Swede who doesn't speak Finnish, but that doesn't change a thing – there are none of those girls at this hotel regardless. It's true that the Kungla Hotel does have a bar which looks like the West to tourists from Moscow and Leningrad (since their understanding of what the West looks like largely comes from Russian films where the action takes place overseas, a significant number of which were filmed in Tallinn). But that probably doesn't hold any attraction for you, since it's hardly likely that you have come to Tallinn to sit in a dimly lit drinking den with 1970s interior design.

In short: there is nothing here.

The real reason your decision to stay in this hotel causes questions in the relevant departments is because it lacks something important which the other hotels have: this hotel only recently received authorisation to accommodate foreign tourists, so there is no eavesdropping equipment here. There apparently isn't even any equipment in the bar because during the last renovation, instructions reportedly came from the Communist Party Central Committee to leave the place alone so that party functionaries could come here and relax undisturbed.

But if you are a citizen of the Kingdom of Sweden, then the relevant departments will start to ask questions. Especially if you are a television reporter, your name is Kenneth Lindblom, and you have just recently filmed a story about a large meeting of writers, artists, composers and other so-called intellectuals which took place in Toompea Castle with the connivance of some of the local authorities, during which people gave the current regime a piece of their mind. Then they will surely want to know why the hell you have chosen to stay in this central hotel which lacks the necessary equipment. Isn't it blindingly obvious?

Kenneth Lindblom was in a splendid mood. He'd just finished doing a long interview with Heinz Valk, who had made it very clear what he meant when he said "we are sure to win in the end". True, he'd only recorded the sound, but he had a whole stack of photographs in his briefcase, including a couple from the heritage protection festival in Tartu, of a torchlit procession of students bearing the blue, black and white colours of the Estonian flag. Not together as one flag, but the message was clear enough.

What would you do if you were a television reporter, a citizen of the Kingdom of Sweden and in a splendid mood? Maybe you would have a glass of champagne? Definitely, but that could wait until a little later. An hour or so later at the ferry bar, for example. Right now you might go and have a walk instead. And that is exactly what Kenneth Lindblom does. In any case, he has one more thing he needs to take care of before heading to the harbour.

Two years ago, when he first visited Tallinn, he could not

have dreamt of such a thing. A year ago he would have certainly been wary, even if he'd heard a bombshell like that from someone close and trustworthy, to say nothing of some unfamiliar, slightly fanatical activist at the Estonian House in Stockholm. But now he had no doubt at all that the game was worth the candle.

If you don't take risks, you don't get to drink champagne. That was apparently what they said in these parts.

Kenneth headed at a relaxed pace through Pasatski park in the direction of the town centre, along the road he might have walked down if he'd been staying at Viru Hotel as he was supposed to. He'd walked down this road before, but this time he was especially interested in the trees – or to be precise, in one particular tree. He knew very well where that tree was situated, even though he'd obviously left the map of the park, with its paths, benches and a red mark in a certain spot, back in Stockholm.

He looked around, didn't see anything suspicious, stepped off the path, and shoved his hand into the hollow of the tree.

It was empty.

Which you could no longer say of the spot next to Kenneth.

"Damned fool!" said the man behind the table. He was prone to corpulence but otherwise in good physical shape, and had turned red in the face from anger. His words were aimed at his colleague, who was a fair bit younger than him, and junior in rank. He'd just reported on the Swede, and was now sitting across the table, hunched up as small as possible. "You damned stupid bastard!"

"I didn't get there in time, Comrade Major," said the younger man, trying to explain. "I was just too late."

That was the truth. As soon as he'd made sure of what was in the envelope, he'd started to head back, planning to place the envelope back into the tree hollow. But when he arrived he found the Swede already there. Of course there was no doubt what he was looking for. Just like there was no reason to suppose that he would ever be given a visa to visit the Soviet Union again. But since the Swede had sussed out what was going on with lightning speed and had jumped back on to the path like a frightened deer, it was unfortunately not possible to accuse him of spying, clap him in irons and deliver him to the KGB building on Pagari Street. In the current climate something like that could cause an international scandal: the security organs would be accused of baseless harassment of a foreign journalist in search of a scoop. And Major Vinkel would not have that.

And so at first they did not know precisely who this person was, or what exactly was going on. Nor did they know how it was all being orchestrated from abroad.

Naturally Kenneth Lindblom was thoroughly searched at the port. Naturally he had to part with the photos of the blue, black and white flag, and a whole shipload of passengers had to wait while his interview with Heinz Valk was listened to, in an office which was assigned for such purposes. In the end they didn't take that from him, but then it wasn't so significant without the photographs. In the ship's bar he ordered brandy instead of champagne. Two brandies. It had been one of those days.

Meanwhile, Major Vinkel was sitting lost in thought.

He'd long since suspected that those guys with the banners weren't as innocent as they appeared, but he hadn't suspected that there could be a thread leading directly from them to foreign intelligence agencies (who else could be behind all this?). He wasn't as paranoid as his comrades in Moscow who, to put it figuratively, saw the long arm of the CIA behind every sloppily tied Pioneer neckerchief. But then nor was he as naïve as some of that new lot in the Party Central Committee who thought that letting critically minded poets go on foreign trips presented absolutely no danger to the socialist order, rather that it showed the Party in a better light because it was open to rational dialogue. Major Vinkel knew very well that every one of us was a soldier on the battlefield of an information war, and that in the end the outcome of the war would not be decided by the number of tanks or nuclear warheads, but by the strength of the trenches which were dug into people's minds – although he also had to concede that the ideological work they'd been doing for a couple of decades now hadn't produced the expected results. Kryuchkov had visited from Moscow, lectured the locals, made a real dog's dinner of things, and now they had to lap up the consequences. How could the people in Moscow not understand that all that stuff was grist for the Americans' mill? If you really want to tighten the screws, then give us a decent screwdriver to do it with, damn it!

In general, Vinkel favoured a fair but firm approach. He didn't do the interrogations himself, as he knew that he was likely to fly off the handle and start shouting at the suspect. For that same reason, they didn't tend to let him report to the senior bosses. But he had no equal when it came to planning, analysis and coordination of operations. He knew that himself. And as a professional in his field he could appreciate how well his colleagues handled the interrogations. Take for example Yevstigneyev, or now that Särg too, whom Fyodor Kuzmich had assigned to help him from the sixth department, which investigated economic crimes. They knew how to talk to suspects calmly and patiently – not like Ots or Zhukov, who would always resort to harsher methods too quickly, such as, for example, dispatching suspects to Seewald mental hospital for electric shock treatment. In Vinkel's view those kinds of tactics were tantamount to admitting defeat, but then he wasn't in the habit of criticising his juniors if there was no absolute need to. If the desired results were not achieved, for example... An American president had once said that he who can, does, and he who cannot, teaches. Those Americans had hit the nail right on the head on that point, at least.

It's hard to say how many of us had one of those people who was prone to corpulence but otherwise in good shape situated somewhere on the outer edges of our social circle, but it's safe to say that plenty of us did. The kind of person you might meet at a distant relative's wedding and talk to at length about fishing, or at some garden party, where he somehow popped up quite unexpectedly, but was very welcome because of his barbecue skills. Or because he could expertly explain why the Zhiguli 07 was a significantly better car than the 05. Some of them might have sailed for a hobby, or gone with their wives to the Sõprus cinema, followed by Gloria restaurant. Because they had their lives to live as well, did they not? They somehow had to exist in the same world as the rest of us – to eat, love, sleep and shit. To yearn and to fear. But where did they come from? How did they explain to themselves who they were, and justify what they did? Surely they had to explain it in some way? A more disturbing question is what these people would have done if our history had turned out differently, more happily. The majority of them would still have been here somewhere, wouldn't they? It can't have been that the Soviet system, which held so many people in fear, could have survived for so long just because a sufficient number of our fellow citizens were moral scum, cynics, sadists and dregs of society, who desired nothing more than to cut their betters down to size. Because it's surely not possible that those people who had a much better idea of what was going on, certainly more than an orangutan's inkling, could have seriously believed what was written in the textbooks of scientific communism.

Or did they largely mix with their own kind? Believing that they were somehow cut from a better cloth. They probably had neighbours, but not friends? Perhaps they were proud of their own professionalism and thought that even if the system which they were helping to keep afloat was not ideal, it was at least preferable to the chaos which would inevitably ensue if it were not for them? Or maybe it was all a kind of rough sport for them, a chess game against invisible opponents, with human fates at stake instead of chess pieces. Or were they really of the view that the rulers of this world were incorrigible brutes and pigs, much the same wherever you went, and that it was a mistake to believe that some leaders could be better than others according to some kind of objective principle: that was just the honey-tongued propaganda of the enemy. The Russian authorities, which have always brazenly plundered the country's riches, silencing any opposition with a heavy blunt object, have systematically tried to convince their smarter citizens of that point, and they do so to this day. Everyone else is at it, so why not me too, or so the logic goes. And if it repeatedly proves necessary to slam some confused citizen's fingers in the desk drawer, it might not be pretty, but there's nothing else for it. Could it even be that when a security operative gives up some part of his humanity in the name of the common good, he is making a tough but benevolent sacrifice which releases him from any higher-order responsibility?

Or maybe they didn't give it much thought so long as they could keep their cosy jobs and put bread on the table. I don't know.

Unlike many of my older colleagues my encounters with the KGB were only fleeting. They tried to recruit me a couple of times at university. One time I expressed myself a little too frankly to my fellow students and one of them reported me, so I was invited to the Komsomol Committee where I was presented with various denunciatory letters, including from people whom I'd considered to be friends. But I was already expecting that, since quite a few of them had come to see me about it beforehand. They told me that they'd been forced into it, but that they'd tried to write in such a way that nothing too bad would come of it. Others kept quiet. One of them refused to write anything, although he didn't tell me that himself; I found out later from other sources. Maybe because the person who reported on me was his roommate. I was seriously afraid, because the man who conducted the correctional discussion with me was known to be connected to the KGB. Although it seemed that my case was initially just an internal matter for the university, and my academic supervisor stood up for me. At that time our department was headed by a very elderly Jewish professor who had spent her best years in a Stalinist labour camp, where she'd been sent after the regime had executed her first husband. He was a Japanese communist who had somehow ended up in the workers' paradise and was naturally accused of being a spy by the paranoid Soviet authorities. By now she'd remarried and after that incident I started to be a frequent guest at her pleasant home; I still have some of the old editions of Japanese classics which she gave me. But that's another story. The KGB recruiters wouldn't leave me in peace, and I had to endure a couple more conversations like that during my university years. The last one to try was someone who introduced himself as Valent Kirilovich (name unchanged) from the KGB headquarters on Liteyniy Avenue in Leningrad, who had an intellectual demeanour and an athletic build. In the end he had to content himself with me writing down his phone number and promising that I would call if I ever felt like talking. Of course we both knew I wouldn't. I only saw him once after that, when Rosita and I were travelling by metro in St Petersburg (we were not yet married, but she already knew all these stories). We were sitting facing the doors and there he was, boarding at some station somewhere in the middle of our journey, and then standing at the end of the carriage. I tried not to look in his direction. After a couple of stops he got off.

"You know who that was?" I started to say.

"I know," Rosita replied.

But unfortunately your file follows you wherever you go; you can't escape it. After I finished university I worked as head of the literature section at Tallinn Puppet Theatre for a few years. One day my desk phone rang and a male voice introduced himself, in Russian, as a member of staff at the Chamber of Commerce and Industry, and said he would like to meet me because I spoke Japanese and a few other foreign languages. I said that I wasn't interested, my field was the humanities, and commerce and industry were foreign to me. "What do you mean you're not interested?" he asked, getting worked up. "We could even send you abroad for a bit … we only want a quick chat, what could you have against that?" I'd already had some contact with the Chamber of Commerce and Industry, but for some reason he didn't know about that; evidently information didn't travel so well there either. I'd once helped out on a visit of some prospective investors from Japan who were interested in the Mistra carpet factory. So I remembered meeting one member of staff from the chamber and I knew that they had quite a different manner. But I didn't say that to the man who was talking to me in Russian, and so he simply told me an address and the time I was expected there. When I approached the place, which was up on Toompea, I spotted a Volga car parked a little way from the front door, with the engine running and three men sitting inside. I reckon they were waiting for me. But I managed to quickly slip in through the door and head to my acquaintance's office, who knew nothing of a supposed meeting with me, and thought that I might have been lured out of my house so that someone could burgle me blind – such things were known to happen. I asked her to call me a taxi, and when it arrived at the front door I ducked into it and drove off. The Volga didn't follow.

In brief

This is me, right here and right now: I am a fifty-three-year-old man, husband and father of two. I am overweight, and from time to time I try to do something about it, but then I stop bothering again. I still take an interest in what is going on in the world. I have been lucky in life, I know that. I am surrounded by people whom I love. I enjoy my work, and my salary is sufficient. I have seen the world. My family wants for nothing. It is people just like me who think up those theories about us living in the best of possible universes – even if there is a lot of unfairness, there could be much more if things were different. I have plans, and I hope to fulfil them. I still feel happy when someone I don't know praises something I have done, and I am sad if one of my friends tells me honestly that he thinks that my work is not up to standard. But I would rather be sad than live without those kinds of friends.

So then, I soon got another call from that man, and I recognised him by his voice again but this time he introduced himself as a member of staff from the State Security Committee called Oleg Makin (name unchanged), and said that he would like to discuss some matters of mutual interest. And perhaps I could suggest a café where our meeting might take place.

I said that he could come to see me at work at the Puppet Theatre. And so they came. Before they arrived I told everyone that if they wanted to see some real live KGB operatives, they would have a chance to very soon.

There were two of them. Both of them were wearing long leather coats. Oleg Makin and an Estonian who introduced himself as Viktor. Maybe his name really was Viktor, who knows. They didn't have anything on me, although obviously they raised the subject of anti-regime views right away, to which I just said look at the newspapers, comrades: it was already 1987 and Gorbachev's perestroika and glasnost were in full swing. So the only thing that they could throw at me was that I'd discerned the Party's new line before the Party itself. Then they told me that young people sometimes get carried away and need protecting against their own passions, and who better than the KGB to provide that service, as long as we know who, what, where and how. So it wouldn't be a bad thing to meet at some café from time to time, because it's good for us intellectuals to talk now and then. As we spoke various actors from the Puppet Theatre looked in through the door intermittently and giggled, which really annoyed my interlocutors. Eventually they realised that they weren't going to get anything from me.

I saw Viktor several times again some years later, after Estonia had regained independence. He was working as a security guard and doorman at one of the embassies in Tallinn, a job which consisted of letting in people one by one from the queue for visas of dozens if not hundreds standing in the corridor. I had no idea whether the embassy knew about his record of public service, nor was it any of my business.

But I saw him, and I knew that he knew.

And he saw me, and he knew that I knew.

Nowadays we talk about grass-roots organisations, local committees, neighbourhood watch.

Nowadays we would say: why don't you set up a non-profit organisation, apply for project funding, get yourself a website, you're bound to get some interesting proposals.

But back then it was simply called the youth recreation room, under the auspices of the district housing service. Because of course it had to be administratively "under" something, and be given a name, to make it official.

The explanation was actually somewhat simpler: two fathers had been wondering what to do about their increasingly unruly children, and so they decided to roll up their sleeves and tidy up the large cellar under the house, which basically belonged to everyone and no one. They used all the means at their disposal and equipped it with a billiards table and carom board, and some other board games which didn't take up much space, like chess and draughts. And two pairs of dumb-bells: one quite light, the other heavier. And a medicine ball. Against one of the walls they put a bookshelf with back issues of the magazines *Thunder* and *Youth*.

Those were actually pretty decent magazines.

And so the unruly children now had a place to go. As did their friends. And sometimes their friends' friends. There was the usual smell of damp and plaster in the cellar, but that didn't bother them. It was more important that no one was checking up on them. And they kept order in their territory themselves: once when two of the newer boys produced two bottles of Azerbaijani fortified wine from their school bags, they were politely asked to leave and never show themselves there again.

Indrek was the first to arrive. Fortunately he knew where the key was hidden. They had started locking the cellar a while back – sometimes from the inside as well. They still played billiards there just as before, but it was not the most important thing any more.

And for several years now some printed materials with quite a different subject matter had started to accumulate amongst the back copies of those aforementioned magazines. They came as seven typed carbon copies on sheets as thin as cigarette paper. They covered the Molotov-Ribbentrop Pact and the Otto Tief government, and revealed that it was in fact the blue, black and white flag of Estonian independence, not the Nazi swastika, which the Red Army lieutenant Lumiste had taken down from Tall Hermann Tower at the end of the war. They also covered the deportations of Estonians to Siberia. By now newspapers and journals were gradually starting to write about these things too, so those were collected and kept here as well. But the cellar door was still kept locked, just in case.

Once Raim had arrived Indrek told him all the details, starting with the two men from the café, up until Pasatski Park and the black car which had taken Karl away.

"Damned fucking hell," said Raim.

That wasn't typical of him.

What could a KGB file tell you about a puny young man in his late twenties?

Everything, or nothing at all, depending on how you looked at things. Captain Särg preferred to assume that it said nothing at all.

He knew that the man called Karl sitting on the stool across the table was feeling edgy, that his mouth was dry. But that was more or less all that he knew for certain. Because what was in the file might turn out to be of no significance at all, it was just numbers and words until they found the key, the missing link which joined up all the pieces, which enabled the mosaic to be assembled into a picture.

Särg knew very well that it might take some time, but eventually the key was sure to be found. They were unlikely to succeed at the first attempt. If this was the first time that the young man the other side of the table had been caught doing something illegal, if his fear was the abstract kind – the fear that in the eyes of the wider world he was suddenly no longer who he'd been before – then it would have been a different story. Then perhaps some sympathetic support would have been enough, a helping hand outstretched to someone who had slipped up. But this one here was different: he'd already made his choice. So what if this was his first time at their place.

Very well.

"You do understand why you are here?" Särg asked.

Silence. Just his gaze.

"Is it true that you work, or worked, in the transport department of the Union of Consumer Cooperatives of the Estonian Soviet Socialist Republic?"

"What do you mean 'worked'? I'm still there."

Now it was Särg's turn to be silent and hang his head, to make sure that Karl understood what would happen to him if his employer was informed – so that he knew his whole former life had now closed behind him, like a wound which has healed over.

But Karl was thinking about something else altogether. How

could they have messed up so badly? Up until today he was certain that everything had been going just fine. He and the lads would talk about the spots of bother they got into almost as if they were boasting: who had a black Volga parked outside their window for hours on end with two dour-faced men sitting inside it smoking, who had been taken aside for crossing on a red light and instead of completing a normal statement had to spend several hours sitting in the cop shop on Lubja Street, just so that he knew that they could do whatever they wanted with him, whenever they wanted, any which way they wanted. But nothing like this had happened before. He didn't visit the cellar any more, just in case it was being watched. But he lived in the same block as Tarts's grandmother, and he met the rest of them at her place. And it simply wasn't conceivable that Tarts's grandmother's flat was bugged. It would be hard to find a more harmless old woman. And Tarts only went to sleep there when his mother had drunk herself senseless with her latest lover, but that didn't happen very often.

Karl knew very well that he was no hero. But in the bottom of his heart he didn't want to admit to himself that those so-called dangerous assignments, which were supposed to put him to the test, actually involved no real danger. Until this moment.

"Do you actually know what was in the envelope?" Särg asked.

"What envelope?" Karl asked back.

At that moment the door opened and a woman slightly over thirty entered. She had a dark complexion, but light blue eyes, and coal-black hair which curled coquettishly upwards just before reaching her shoulders.

"Here are those typed-up statements which you asked for," she said in Russian.

There was no doubt at all – she knew that she was very beautiful.

Her name was Lidia Petrovna Gromova.

Remember her.

Other people had names like Volli, Yevgeny and Anton, or Galina, Maarika and Lembe but Särg himself had always been simply Särg.

Actually his parents had given him the fairly uncommon name Helmut, which the teachers and children at kindergarten used for a while, but things changed from his very first day at school. It just so happened that there was another Helmut in his class, and as fate would have it this Helmut was one of those uncommon boys who were both sporty and bright, the kind who had the whole school hanging on their every word. And so he soon asserted his monopoly over that first name.

What's more, Särg was easy to say. And there were no other children whose names meant a type of fish.[1]

From an early age Särg had learned to weigh up risks and opportunities rationally and as they arose, so he did not take offence. Only his mother continued to call him Helmut, which at first was touching, but then became simply strange (his father preferred a simpler form of address: "boy, damn it"). Once he'd started at the university's law department he introduced himself to everyone using his short surname and a similarly brisk handshake.

> ### Grandad
>
> *Some time I would like to write about my grandfather at greater length, but now is not the time. I don't mean the one who wrote poetry, got into trouble repaying his bank loan, and departed with the Russians during the war. I mean the other one, who never lived to see me, who trained to become a field nurse under tsarism, travelled by train to Manchuria on a humanitarian mission to fight the plague, and was then steward on an armoured*

---

1   Translator's note: *Särg* means "roach" in Estonian.

train during the War of Independence (it wasn't that trains were an obsession of his, in case you got that impression). So then, that particular grandfather apparently once said that he never read storybooks, because he could think up anything which he might find in them for himself. So he only ever wanted to read about real things.

Let's leave aside the question of whether it is possible to write about real things, or whether everything is to some extent imagined. Of course it is, but there is still a difference, as I'm sure you will appreciate.

Clearly I don't agree with him on the subject of storybooks, otherwise I wouldn't write them myself. But it is still worth asking: is there actually any sense in inventing security service officials and dissidents, and even making them a little different to how they really were? After all, there are still plenty of real people around who lived through all of that stuff themselves; why not just listen to them instead? I don't have much to say in my defence, other than that I am doing the best I can.

By that time his lank hair had started to show the first signs of thinning down the middle, and the lenses in his black-rimmed glasses were thicker than the maximum permitted for military service, which meant he was allowed to resit the university entrance exams when he failed them at the first attempt. He spent the intervening time doing low-paid work in the district Komsomol Committee; it would look good on his CV, even if it had no ideological content. Indeed, it achieved the desired effect: even though he himself evaluated his performance as weaker, since he'd forgotten some things over the course of the year, his exam results turned out better the second time round. Over the years he'd come to be grateful that people tended not to notice his presence, which meant he could observe them from a distance, and he eventually became something of an expert judge of character. It was just a shame that he didn't know how to turn that skill to any practical use.

To start with, that is. Once assigned to the role of investigator at the Procurator's Office, he soon discovered he was far better at squeezing information from suspects during interrogations than any of his colleagues. What was more, the suspects themselves were often completely unaware he was doing so. And so he soon found himself being entrusted with more and more important cases. He was particularly useful in situations where quick calculations were needed, since he had a natural way with numbers. But he found that tracking down larger-scale financial machinations left him completely cold. It was as if these sums came from another world, qualitatively different from the smooth, fresh notes which the cashier handed him through the small window in the thick blue wall on payday, after he'd waited ages in the queue to sign his name. More important than the numbers themselves was the ingenuity of the riddle and the joy he experienced at finding a neat solution which left no threads hanging. But he could only remember feeling a deep sense of satisfaction from his work on one occasion. That was when he succeeded in putting his former classmate behind bars for a long stretch. It was that damned other Helmut, who was now a petrol station manager and an embezzler of state resources on a major scale. Again, it was down to Särg that Helmut decided to cooperate with the investigation – and he was wise to do so since back in those days he could've faced the death sentence for what he'd done.

That case didn't go unnoticed up above. One day two men in plain clothes came to Särg's office, introducing themselves only once they'd locked the door behind them. Half an hour had passed before they opened it again, furnished with Särg's agreement to swap his current role for a new position which would be more challenging, where he would be properly valued for his contribution. It was not often that someone in the legal system was prepared to deal so cold-bloodedly with a childhood friend. Or rather with his namesake.

The change of job came at exactly the right time for Särg. He'd been a family man for several years now, but recently he'd noticed certain signs of restlessness from his wife. There were still no real grounds to worry, but with his innate common sense and powers of empathy, Särg knew that he had to do something.

His marriage to Galina had come about very soon after they met. At one of the office parties he paused to have a chat with the girl from accounts with the distinctive shock of blonde hair, and to his surprise he ended up seeing her home, all the way to the fifth floor of the block of flats in Mustamäe where she lived. Galina then rode him so vigorously for half the night that Särg was surprised at his own stamina. And at how interested the girl seemed to be in him. Since the next day was Saturday, neither of them had to hurry anywhere. Once out of bed, however, Särg was a little embarrassed to discover that Galina's elderly mother had clearly had no choice but to listen to their moaning and groaning from her neighbouring room. Once they were properly introduced she assured Särg that her age notwithstanding she slept very well, although she struggled to stifle a yawn as she spoke. As an experienced interrogator Särg could draw the obvious conclusions. In any case, his future mother-in-law Varvara Sergeyevna had already made them a hearty plateful of fried eggs and rashers of bacon, which she'd just bought fresh from the market. There was a sports programme of some sort on TV, and Särg had to pretend to be interested since it had been put on especially for him. Then he and Galina went to the park and walked hand in hand for a while. He was invited to stay for lunch as well but decided that it would be politer to decline.

The following month was probably the only time in his life that Särg's conviction that people were essentially machines driven by their desires and fears was shaken. Särg had no idea at all what the real state of affairs was – that Galina's period was already quite late and that the likely culprit, one Yevgeny, no longer wanted anything to do with her. A couple of days later in the canteen he casually sat down at Galina's table with his plate of pork chops and glass of compote, having in fact waited for her for some time there. Galina's friend quickly left, and they agreed that they would go to the cinema that very same day to watch a film about which they later remembered nothing at all. It probably had some kind of psychological subject matter. When it transpired a few days later that Varvara Sergeyevna was going to be staying at a sanatorium in Haapsalu for two weeks, Särg went back to his rented room to fetch a toothbrush, shaving gear and a couple of changes of underwear, after which he had no reason to go back there for the whole two weeks. He was gradually overcoming the awkwardness that had at first prevented him from reciprocating when Galina touched him so tenderly in all the right places. Särg hadn't exactly been starved of sex in his former life, but he'd always had the common sense to settle for second best and so he'd never felt particularly moved by any of his encounters. Meanwhile Galina found it easy to convince him that their sexual compatibility was down to a special bond between them, not the experience she'd gained from years of practice.

But when one morning Galina's dilemma unexpectedly resolved itself (human biology can work in weird and wonderful ways) and her feelings for Särg suddenly seemed to cool, Särg interpreted this in his own way, put his best suit on, bought ten red roses and a bottle of champagne, and took the bus to Mustamäe. His heart was pounding uncontrollably and he'd not slept a bit the previous night. Galina asked for a little time to think things over, but by now Galina's mother, who had arrived back from the sanatorium, had taken a liking to Särg – he was a polite and decent young man, and even though he didn't drink himself, he would always be sure to fill the ladies' glasses. After having tried drinking a couple of times Särg had indeed decided that he would be best off living without alcohol. He'd noticed that one shot would make him unpleasantly edgy, that he needed a second and third shot to help with that, and after the third all sorts of ideas which he would normally not countenance started to seem sensible to him.

After weighing up her options Galina said yes to Särg. Anton was born a little less than a year after their wedding, and looked exactly like Särg. The young family were allocated a flat, and they managed to swap that and Galina's mother's flat for a very pleasant three-room place in Keldrimäe, where they now lived. By now Särg could no longer imagine his life without Russian borscht and stuffed cabbage.

Galina's maternity leave had come to an end and Särg's mother-in-law was managing fine looking after little Anton. And it could be said that even with his rational view of the human character, Särg had come to understand his nearest and dearest better.

But all that Särg told his wife was that he was transferring to slightly different work. The most important difference was that they could now treat themselves to a holiday in Poland, and Särg had already put them on the waiting list.

The cases which Särg had to investigate in his new role were generally much like the previous ones, only larger in scale, more sophisticated, and wider in scope, and therefore more interesting. Another advantage was that he now got far fewer calls from on high advising him "perhaps you shouldn't follow so and so's lead quite so zealously, if you get my point…" If there were cases where a policeman or even a colleague from those same security organs

43

got nabbed, then they wouldn't be let off the hook. Of course the cases never reached court: the individuals in question would just disappear. No one knew exactly where to. Maybe Barnaul, or Chimkent, or Naryan-Mar – places where they would never have gone of their own volition, but would now be living to the end of their days. Sometimes they would go to work as guards in the prison camps, having saved themselves from becoming prisoners by agreeing to go for longer. Sometimes they were even sent down for the sins of their children, like those loutish Interior Ministry officers whose sons set light to Sassi-Jaan barn and Niguliste church.

Särg had need of his innate mathematical abilities quite often now, because the money which unseen hands dragged into crooked schemes tended to be converted into foreign currency and then back into roubles, and obviously not at the rate set by the Soviet Foreign Trade Bank. Särg also quickly acquired a thorough knowledge of icons, tsarist gold coins and other things which the underworld elite considered held their value well. Of course he knew the hourly rate of the prostitutes in various Tallinn hotels, and how much the bars there charged for different types of tipple, including Viru Valge vodka and Vana Tallinn liqueur, although naturally they could be bought in the shop round the corner for no more than a tenth of the price. But that was all another world for him, which he was happy to observe as if through a window, without feeling the slightest desire to enter it.

By now he was earning enough that Galina didn't need to go back to work, but for Galina the work itself had always been the least interesting aspect of her job. She needed people around her to discuss the ways of the world; she needed someone to impress with some new make-up or matching outfit and jewellery, since the men in her life certainly didn't know how to appreciate such things. And Särg promised that she would now be able to spend her whole salary on herself, since at the end of the month there was always housekeeping money left over in the red and white polka-dot "Cocoa" box.

However, Galina didn't want to go back to work at the Procurator's Office. The atmosphere there was too strict, and there were too many people who still remembered her previous lifestyle. So after a brief search she found herself a cushy job in the Tallinn offices of Aeroflot. The mood was much more pleasant than her previous place, and the job meant she could get hold of tickets to places like Simferopol, Tuapse and Mineralnye Vody – not just for her own family, but for a seamstress friend, her hairdresser, and the head of department in the furniture shop, who in turn arranged for a decent corner sofa to finally arrive in their living room. And it wasn't completely without importance that at her new job Galina didn't have to encounter a single document written in Estonian.

Because no, she couldn't speak that language. Which still bothered Särg a little.

She had the utmost respect for the Estonian people and their culture of course. "Kalevipoeg", Tammsaare and all that. And the Song Festival. And unlike most in her circle of acquaintances she could say, "How's it going?" and "Well, thanks" with a quite acceptable Estonian accent, and she could understand the numbers up to one hundred when a shopkeeper used them. But the rest of it was completely beyond her; there was no point in pretending otherwise.

"Anyway, a woman's language skills aren't her most important quality," she would say coquettishly to Särg, to which he had no choice but to concur. They managed just fine, after all. Särg's Russian had got much better from constant practice. What bothered him more was that their son Anton's first words were in his mother's and grandmother's language, whereas he responded to anything his father said with funny cute noises which his wife's side of the family said sounded exactly like Estonian, and made them laugh heartily. Which Anton of course took as encouragement.

They rarely visited Särg's parents in the countryside; he knew very well that he could never bring himself to tell his father where he was now working.

Anton did not in fact learn to speak Estonian as a child at all. Särg's working days were long and he often had to be away at weekends, so he played a modest part in his son's upbringing. In any case, whenever he did have some free time Galina would claim it for herself, and they would go to Sõprus cinema and then to Gloria restaurant for dinner, since Särg's mother-in-law was quite happy to look after Anton. All four of them would go on holiday to the Crimea together, where they always rented two rooms, and Anton would be in one of them with Grandma.

The problems started when Anton got older, when he began playing outdoors and found himself caught between two camps. He was in the same predicament at school. Anton attended Middle School No. 47, where they were fostering friendship between the peoples by having the Estonian and Russian classes together in one building, with a full set of teachers for every subject in each language. Anton didn't mix with the Estonian boys, and while the Russians tolerated his presence they didn't treat him as one of their own because of his surname. Anyway, they needed someone to tease, and he fitted the role very well. In fact that probably wasn't because of his name, but because he was short in stature, just like his father wore thick-rimmed glasses due to his poor eyesight, and wasn't particularly sporty. The main thing was that he would never tell on them to teacher. Anton himself saw things differently of course. He didn't understand why being a little bit Estonian was such a problem for the playground bullies. Nor why he always had to play the role of fascist in their war games.

> *If we always knew in advance what was going to happen, we would behave like machines. So in a sense it is the unexpected things in life that make us who we are.*

But what doesn't kill you makes you stronger, as they say.

As a teenager Anton gradually grew further apart from his parents. Their world was of no interest to him, nor did he want to share his world with them. But his parents saw no cause for worry: his marks were good and he was even sent to take part in the Estonian Soviet Republic's Physics Olympiad – although he'd actually started to get more interested in history, especially after his two history teachers, the Estonian one and the Russian one, had a shouting match in the staffroom that nearly came to blows. And by now he'd begun studying Estonian diligently, although he still found it difficult, and he didn't use it at home with his father. To be honest, he didn't speak much with his father at all.

Anyway, what would a true Estonian man have to say to a Russified spook?

It had already gone five when Ervin, Tarts and Pille appeared through the cellar door; Anton had to go straight home. They didn't know what Indrek wanted to tell them, so they'd kept him waiting. They were in a jolly mood when they arrived since their collection jar had ended up quite full by the end of the day, much fuller than the previous week.

"It started raining in the end," Tarts said. "We'll probably have to make some new posters. And paint some new freckles on to Ervin." They all laughed. At least they now had enough money to buy some card and paints.

Once they had heard out Indrek and Raim they realised that they had much bigger problems on their hands. Things were pretty bad. But then, although they didn't forget their friend for a moment, the customary tone started to return to their conversation: that jaunty banter, that self-belief. If only they could believe it within themselves, then they really could be free, right here and right now.

Ervin looked at his friends – because they were still his friends, despite everything that had happened – and experienced a feeling which was strange but not exactly unpleasant. He was the only one in that room who knew that there was now an invisible line running between them, separating them from each other. Of course he knew that what he'd done could not possibly fit into their shared conception of right and wrong. And, believe it or not, he still wanted to belong to their group, to be one of the few who dared to stand up and say how things really were, to proclaim the imminent arrival of freedom, in which no one would be imprisoned over their convictions or force-fed through a tube when they went on hunger strike. Or at least part of Ervin felt like that. The other part, which normally showed itself at night, or when he was hung-over, was quite sure that their activities were hopeless and pointless, that the enemy was tolerating them just for the sake of

48

appearances. Because the enemy knew it could crush them flat as soon as it deemed necessary. Shave off Ervin's red locks and chuck him into a dingy cell or send him to Siberia, from where he would return a different person. Ervin knew that would be a senseless sacrifice, and he was not prepared to make it. Anyway, what kind of nation entrusted the struggle for independence to a handful of young lads, who had still not learned to stand upright, to say nothing of falling in love, or mourning the dead. And what kind of nation then skulks off to its comfortable-enough den, its soft-enough bed, under its warm-enough blanket, to watch their struggle from a distance. He envied those friends who were prepared to stand to the last, and he wished he felt the same way. But there was nothing he could do. That's just how things were. And it was now especially strange to listen to their joshing, after what he'd done today. This was no longer his world. Of course, when Madisson and then Bötker were exiled to Sweden, he realised that the career of a freedom fighter could actually conclude quite pleasantly. Why not follow them there? And if, contrary to any logic, things were to turn out as his wonderful, naïve friends thought – intoxicated as they were by their collective self-deception – and some sort of Estonian Republic were to make a comeback, then at least he would have made a contribution. As well as standing in the picket, he'd drawn swastikas on Soviet statues at night and had been on lookout duty a couple of times when Hangman's gang went to nick the wheels off the commies' cars. Just like that night when they were caught – and he was offered the chance of getting off more lightly.

It wasn't as if he didn't sometimes get the urge to admit everything to the others. They were his friends after all, they would understand, they would forgive him, fuck Sweden, we'll go there some time later, they would say. And anyway, they could use the situation Ervin had got himself into to further the cause. The KGB now trusted him and could be fed all sorts of rubbish, be steered on to any old idiots, who would find themselves at the headquarters on Pagari Street instead of him and his friends.

But no. Ervin stayed quiet, in an exemplary fashion.

He still does.

I remember one time back in 1988 (or was it 1989?): I was reading some information about the freedom movement on the wall by the Pegasus café when I came across the name of a man I had once fleetingly encountered a dozen or so years previously, back at middle school, when I took an interest in Esperanto. Let's say this was him: clean-shaven but with a thick head of hair, chubby, his cheeks always rosy, which gave him a rather comical and utterly benign appearance – like the funny friend of the protagonist in romantic films, or the sad clown in the circus.

In the end he didn't quite succeed in becoming a politician.

And he is dead now, as I discovered when I tried to track him down.

His name was Valev. He was soft-spoken by nature, but when he got worked up he had the habit of waving his arms about without even noticing he was doing so. He never gave out his own number; he would always phone you.

There were two of them walking along, one of them taller, with broad shoulders and a chin which jutted determinedly forward, he was walking a bit slower. The other was older, shorter, but more edgy and animated, evidently his companion's mentor, the one who was in charge. They walked back and forth along the road between the Victory Square underpass and St Charles' Church, making sure that no one was watching in front or behind. Raim was speaking while Valev listened with a worried expression on his face.

"It's a real drag, that's for sure," Valev said, casting a quick glance over his shoulder, "and I hope that Karl bears up. It's going to be really tough for him. I'm afraid that if they don't let him go after a couple of days that means that they're getting properly stuck into him. They're particularly brutal at the moment."

A passer-by looked in their direction and Valev fell silent for a moment.

"Because we've actually won already, you know," he said. "I found out – don't ask how – that an order was sent from Moscow, from the head of the KGB himself, telling them to work out a plan for going underground. Including cover stories for their own people and contact points for transferring funds in the future. And of course a network for blackmail operations."

"Aha," said Raim.

"That means two things," Valev said. His voice almost became a whisper, and his cheeks started to flush. "Firstly, that we'll get our country back, sooner or later. That's certain. No doubt about it any more. But secondly, because there is a secondly as well … if their plan succeeds, we might end up with a maggoty apple. You understand what I mean, an apple full of maggots." Raim thought he could see Valev trying to trace the shape of an apple in the air. "A maggoty apple." Then his arms fell limply on either side of him, he cleared his throat and recovered his voice: "That is if we don't do anything to stop it."

"So what can we do?" Raim asked.

Valev started to explain. He looked around again and then took an object wrapped in yesterday's paper from inside his coat.

It was a miniature camera, originally invented by one Walter Zapp, an engineer of Baltic German extraction who had lived in Tallinn's Nõmme district in 1936 before moving to Riga. Now known as the Minox EC, it had been significantly improved in the intervening years, was being manufactured in Germany, and had earned renown as the world's smallest photographic device, capable nevertheless of producing very high-resolution pictures.

And he also had a name to give Raim. Someone who had been stirred from the silence of the shadows: Gromova.

But now, dear reader, something more pleasant awaits us: let us leave behind this weary land for a while.

This journey is not an easy one, but it is not the first time that we embark on it, and we even have foreign passports for the purpose, kept in a safe place at home. A few years ago the authorities took them away from anyone who had travelled overseas as soon as they got home, with the exception of a few especially trustworthy persons. But in recent times it is no longer so rare for people like us to have our passports in our possession all the time. We have also managed to get hold of multiple-entry Finnish visas, arranged by our old acquaintances from the Friedebert Tuglas Society in Helsinki who have been visiting Estonia for years now, bringing with them coffee, books and tights, together with anything else necessary for a dignified existence. We have known them since we were teenagers, and have practised the Finnish we learned from television with them. The last time we were in Finland we even stayed with them in Espoo, feeling a little embarrassed that we arrived from the event we were at quite late and a little tipsy, although we managed not to wake up their grandchildren.

Fortunately things are a little different this time. We even have our own hotel rooms, and not just in any old hotel, but in the Hesperia (now a Crowne Plaza hotel). We have got ourselves on the guest list for a celebratory reception put on by a Soviet-Finnish joint venture, recently set up with the aim of using Finnish equipment to produce paper for the Soviet Union. Because the Soviet Union has no paper. That is, there is enough for the newspapers, but books sometimes have to wait years to be printed. Although not for much longer, if one is to believe the documents which both parties signed ceremoniously today.

We don't see that happening because the signing event is only meant for the delegates, but we will still get into the party in the evening. Don't worry, we have an official invitation, arranged for us by the same Friedebert Tuglas

Society. Because if there is paper, then books can be published, and that is something which writers will want to celebrate, to say nothing of their readers.

So as the agreement between Director of Karelia Trade Yrjö Paananen and Soviet Minister for Forestry and Timber Mikhail Ivanovich Bussygin, which makes the factory possible, is signed in the Soviet Embassy in Helsinki, and the first chink of champagne glasses rings out, we are still waiting in the customs queue in Tallinn harbour, which is particularly slow today. But it always seems that way. You try to look calm, and you pull it off pretty well, or at least I suspect nothing, but of course you can't fool the customs official. I only have my possessions yanked out of my bags, but you have your pockets searched as well. Thankfully the one-hundred-mark note you got from your cousin is hidden in your sock, and the customs official eventually resigns himself to finding nothing, deciding that the edginess he read on your face was just because of the irksome experience you were being put through, which was of course quite possible. Tomorrow you will take that one-hundred-mark note to the electronics shop on Iso Roobertinkatu Street and use it to buy a "Tallinn kit", which costs forty-two marks and contains a couple of tiny components that your cousin can use to make his new TV set show Finnish television with colour and sound. The same thing would cost several times more on the black market in Tallinn, so your cousin is happy to let you keep the change, but you promise that you will treat him to a glass of the whisky which an acquaintance is going to give you to take home. Anyway, we're now safely up the ramp and on board the ship, which is named after the Estonian singer Georg Ots. We walk about, looking enviously at the Finns and those few Estonians who have bought themselves a beer at the bar. We have alcohol with us as well, but we are taking it to our acquaintances in Finland. Some of the Finns anyway look like they no longer have much need for the bar: they're barely able to stand upright as it is. One of them is making no attempt to hide his interest in the girls in fancy white blouses and denim skirts as they walk past.

Eventually we find one of the ship's dimly lit cafés – too dark to read, but at least the Estonian waitress can pretend that she can't see that we have ordered nothing, and leave us to our own devices, making no claims on our scant supply of hard currency. And so our journey goes, a bit hungrily, thirstily and joylessly, but at least in the right direction. You have brought two apples with you, and you treat me to one of them. Thank you for that. An hour before arrival we take up position by the exit so as to avoid waiting in the queue for too long. The Finns don't have to worry about that, there is a separate queue for them; they must do little more than walk past the border guard with their passports held open. Just in case, you pull the one-hundred-mark note out of your sock before we leave the café; even though our invitation says we will be looked after and our bills paid, the border guard may ask us to show some money. Just to make sure that we remember our place.

As if it were possible to forget.

Reality

Actually, the first time I went to Finland I didn't use this boat: I took the bus through Leningrad and Vyborg and then travelled onwards along the coast. We had to get to a gathering of Finnish and Estonian poets, and the whole thing was nearly called off because Gorbachev had requisitioned the Georg Ots ferry to travel to Reykjavík and meet Ronald Reagan. But we still decided to go.

At one event there, an elderly woman asked me what I found most remarkable about Finland. She said she liked to collect peoples' first impressions, as they gave her a fresh perspective on her homeland. I replied that it was the petrol stations. I explained that when I was a child I had Matchbox cars brought back for me from Finland, and my classmate Peeter Laurits got given loads of Lego bricks. And so we played with them, building miniature models of a reality which was absent from our own lives. Now, years later, it was strange to see the petrol stations there by the roadside, as if a wall between me and my childhood toys had crumbled, as if I had stepped across a dividing line which had been separating me from that reality.

We are met at the harbour; a thin girl asks us to put our cases in the back of a minibus and she takes us to the Hesperia. We hear Estonian spoken from both sides of the foyer, but those girls aren't connected with our delegation: they are wearing expensive clothes and smell of top-quality perfume. When they see us they fall silent, because we bring back memories. We hurriedly take our suitcases to our rooms and put our best clothes on – the reception has already begun. We enter the hall and are separated for a while – just in case, I let you know that the buffet nearest the door is meant for the Soviet delegation and consists mainly of vodka with or without juice, whereas at the other end of the hall you will find a pretty decent selection of wines, and the nibbles are just that little bit better too.

Alex was quite happy with vodka and juice. He felt a little uncomfortable, which was probably why he'd already downed a few drinks and was a bit flushed, but that also may have been due to the crush of people. He didn't know anyone here apart from the Lenbumprom (Leningrad Paper Industry) people, but he couldn't be bothered to talk about work stuff – he could talk about that to his heart's content back home in Leningrad. He'd managed to exchange pleasantries with a couple of young Finns, but the conversations hadn't lasted long as chit-chat wasn't his strong point.

I'll have a plateful of food, a drink or two, and then I'll go to my room, he thought – tomorrow is another day, after all.

Standing in front of him in the queue was a jovial-looking older gentleman wearing spectacles who seemed to know exactly which of the snacks to take and which to leave alone, while for Alex they all remained something of a mystery. Since the man was clearly an expert, Alex decided to let himself be guided by his choices, and so he helped himself to what had probably once been some kind of sea creature, and some lumps of cheese served with pieces of an unidentifiable fruit.

The elderly gentleman took note.

"I take it this is your first time here," he half-asked, half-stated and nodded approvingly in the direction of Alex's plate. His English was a bit stiff, as is often the case with Finns, but that made it easier to understand. "Very good. Now all you need to do is choose the right wine. Come with me."

Alex followed him and listened as he discussed something with the barmaid in Finnish and asked her to fill a couple of large glasses barely quarter-full of lightly sparkling white wine.

"It's from Portugal," the old man explained. "They know their stuff there."

He put his glass and plate down for a moment and took a business card out of his pocket. "Tapani Yläkoski," he read his name out. His place of work, the research department of the Bank of Finland, was also written on the card.

"Pleased to meet you," Alex said in response. "Alex Sushchevsky."

"Let's keep it easy and just use first names," Tapani suggested. "To your health!"

Alex lifted his glass. He discovered that the seafood was actually pretty good. The cheese less so.

It turned out that Tapani had been to Leningrad several

times. Both of them agreed on how rapidly things had improved there recently, and they both hoped the trend could continue.

They decided to have a brandy in honour of that, although Tapani remained a little sceptical about what the future held.

"We've seen it before, when the Kremlin runs out of options," he said. "In Khrushchev's day everyone was full of high hopes too. If Gorbachev takes things too far he'll be put back in his place, that's for sure."

"I don't know," Alex objected. "About five years back I came very close to being thrown out of university. In any case, I had already resigned myself to never being allowed abroad again. But now here I am, I'm even working in one of the new joint ventures."

"So what did you do wrong?" Tapani asked.

"Oh, nothing, it was because of my uncle," Alex said with a dismissive gesture. "He was a mathematician, internationally renowned and all that. Then he jumped ship, went abroad for a conference and didn't come back."

"Is that so?" Tapani mumbled.

"I really hated him for several years," Alex continued. "How could he go and do something like that to us? You've got no idea how seriously they took that kind of thing back then."

"I do actually," Tapani said with a nod. "Things are definitely better now. Has your uncle been to see you since then?"

"He's dead now," Alex answered. "He had cancer. That's why he stayed put in England, I guess. I understand his motivations of course. Not that the treatment would have been better there: we have first-class medical care for people of his standing, always have done. It's just that he didn't want to waste the last years of his life."

"I see."

"He left his homeland a bachelor, but he found himself a

wife there in Oxford, a young one at that," Alex said with a smile. "They travelled round the world together too."

"Fair enough."

"His wife even wrote to me," Alex continued. "And the letter arrived pretty quickly too, only took ten days or so. She said I should come and visit her if I ever get to England. And I will, when the opportunity arises."

"You know what," Tapani said. "My daughter is a journalist, I reckon she'd be pretty interested in your story. What do you think about doing an interview tomorrow? You'll get a small fee for it. And you can talk about your joint venture, what you're up to and all that. What do you say?"

"I'd be happy to," said Alex. A lamp flashed somewhere in the furthermost recesses of his mind, but he turned it off straight away. What was the big deal? So they agreed they would meet outside Kappeli restaurant the following day, and then they ordered another couple of brandies. Not exactly Akhtamar, but it wasn't bad at all.

Alex looked at the Finnish woman sitting opposite him and found himself thinking that she was actually quite attractive, even pretty in her prim Nordic way (if it weren't for the ugly glasses she was wearing), but she looked so awfully naïve, like everyone else from the other side of the Iron Curtain. How could she expect that centuries of tradition, and the fears which had fed them, would disappear overnight, as if brushed aside with the edge of a palm, or that spines which were so used to stooping before their superiors would suddenly straighten and that peoples' heads would turn out to be full of freethinking ideas? Only a few people were capable of changing like that, and it did not come naturally even to them. It was obvious that one had to proceed gradually and cautiously, without upsetting anything, without causing harm to anyone. How could she not understand that people who defended and kept this supposedly evil system artificially alive were not born evil themselves, but were, as far as they and others believed, living to perform their duty, doing their best for the good of society. They'd ended up in a dead end, of course, but people had now started to appear who could lead them out – out of the planned economy, out of Afghanistan, out of the single-party state with no rule of law. That was exactly what was happening, and the pace was head-spinningly fast for some. How could she not realise that?

Silja looked at the Russian sitting opposite her and found herself thinking that he was actually quite attractive, even handsome, in his rough-and-ready Russian way (if it weren't for the ugly tie he was wearing), but he looked so awfully naïve, like everyone else from the other side of the Iron Curtain. How could he believe that it was possible to reform the system from within when it was so ineffective, so completely corrupt, built on irrational and inhumane principles from the very start? To introduce freedoms into peoples' lives, and require that they exercise them responsibly, while the fundamental things remained unchanged. It just wasn't possible. It wasn't possible to be a little bit free, just like you couldn't be a little bit pregnant, and you couldn't take flight with just one wing. Because something would always get in your way: either the realisation that you have to throw off every last one of your chains to really be free, or a painful knock and loss of consciousness after colliding with the brick wall of reality. How could he not realise that?

"Thanks for the interesting conversation," Silja said, taking an envelope out of her handbag and sliding it across the table towards Alex.

"Thank you, I enjoyed it very much too," Alex replied, shoving the envelope into his breast pocket.

Indrek spotted the girls approaching. It was evening, one of those long, sunny, early summer evenings when there was almost no one in town, and no sound other than the harsh grating of the trams as they passed by from time to time. And the occasional car. He saw the girls coming from a distance, so he had some time to observe them. It can sometimes be that the main defining feature of a person, especially a girl, is immediately apparent, even if you can't say exactly what it is. It's like some sort of line, around which everything else revolves, although it is not straight, certainly not straight, and it is unique to that person, some-thing like a DNA spiral, or the graph of a mathematical function. It would be easy to make a model of that person, as long as you had a piece of wire bent in the shape of that line. All you would need to do is add the other stuff, the flesh and bones, but that would just be a matter of finess-ing. This line is not immutable, but the laws which deter-mine how it can bend and in which direction are inherent to it, contained within its curves like an electric charge. Sometimes it is apparent from a girl's legs, for example, or you might realise that her hair is just right, not because she has decided to style it a certain way, but because it reveals this personal line of hers. Indrek knew that if all were well then this line was accompanied by a corresponding sound, conveyed in the girl's voice. The rest was such advanced mathematics, you wouldn't want to trouble yourself with it. Anyway, he should have got to know these girls, but that could never happen. All you need to do is look at them to realise that not only will their uncommonly beautiful per-sonal lines never fully reveal themselves to you, but also that they are in total harmony, that they chime with one another, they reflect and overlap with each other. Because there is some rule which unifies them: for you they are completely, utterly, impossibly unattainable.

They didn't normally come to this part of town, but it was

Helle's birthday today and she'd invited them to Café Moscow after their art class. There were four of them: Tonja, the eldest, with her long dark plait of hair, whose every sentence hung in the air like a question, Maarja with her chiming laughter, Liisi, who was the serious and diligent one, and of course Helle herself, who was the only one to have already got into the Art Institute, and who went to the art evening classes solely to be with her old friends. This evening Helle was in a jovial mood; she'd taken a bottle of champagne to the art class, which they'd drunk right there in the yard, straight out of the bottle. It didn't matter that it had been a little warm, and half of it had ended up on the grass after their lengthy efforts to open it. Helle had brought four painted plastic noses with her, and they were supposed to attach them to their faces with rubber bands and walk through town. As was expected Liisi refused to do so, but the other three put their noses on, took one look at each other and started guffawing. Then the laughter wouldn't leave them, whatever one of them said it caused one of the others to burst out giggling afresh, unrestrainedly, infectiously, for no real reason. The protesters standing on the other side of the road with their serious faces and forlorn placards with slogans like "Freedom for Aare Murakas!" and "Occupying Forces out of Estonia!", whose ink had started to run in the rain, were also pretty funny. But suddenly Maarja's chiming laughter came to an abrupt stop. Of course she found the people there amusing, especially on a day like today, when nothing was off limits. But it still wasn't nice to laugh at them like that. Those guys were standing there for her as well. They stood there day in, day out like a living reproach against all that was wrong with the world, and of course it wasn't their fault that today was the kind of day it was.

"Wait a moment!" Maarja hollered to the others and she handed her folder to Liisi. The first note she found in her pocket was a five-rouble one, which was not actually worth anything any more. She crossed the road and stuffed the note into the glass jar, trying her utmost to contain her laughter. Those funny, taciturn young people had earned it after all.

I probably already mentioned that it was evening by now, and the road was completely free of cars.

Damn that Raim, Indrek thought, when he saw his friend's broad shoulders nudge forward. Some people were happy to look from a distance, but he just goes and takes what he wants (but Indrek was wrong, there was another reason for Raim's behaviour).

Maarja hadn't got back to the other side of the road when one of the young men, a sporty-looking guy with blond hair, probably a few years older than she was, started to run after her.
      "Wait a moment!" he cried out, and Maarja turned round, although she wasn't at all sure if he was addressing her.
      "Come back tomorrow," the young man said, "I've got something I want to tell you."
      That lovely girl, with her button nose, who walked as if she were hovering ten centimetres above the pavement, clearly already had plans for the evening. Anyway he was also busy, he had to go and buy a cake and some flowers, and so forth.
      But that girl could be just right for Valev's plan.

Like a bird's nest

Ever since she was little Maarja had had a strange, almost symbiotic relationship with that creaking two-storey wooden house which was the only place she had ever called home. It was as if they'd grown to be part of one another. When the rain drummed against the tin

---

roof, she felt her hair get wet, and when the sun shone through the windows into the dim kitchen, she squinted. And the same went for the smells. It didn't matter that the house smelt of old people, whenever she got out of the bath she felt as if those smells had faded for awhile. That was why she had always washed herself thoroughly ever since she was little, without ever needing to be told, and she washed her hair more than she needed to too. Later, after Estonia regained independence, after her parents got divorced and she was living in Lasnamäe with her mother, she always came by this house if she was in the Kalamaja area, and since there was no lock on the front door she would always peek inside. When she moved out of her mother's place she wanted to rent a room here, but there were none available. But her memories didn't go anywhere, and haven't to this day. That house no longer physically exists, it was restored to relatives of its original owner who had no links to it; for them all that counted was the location. The disappearance of the house was a blow for Maarja, and it gave her no sense of release, in fact it weighed on her. Not many people would find it easy to go through life dragging a demolished house with them. But all this was still to come. For now those smells are still there, together with the rain and the sun.

Clearly Raim did not ask where Valev had got hold of the information about Lidia Petrovna Gromova, but in the interests of clarity let it be explained. As it happened the source of that information was the same woman from the block where Lidia Petrovna lived, the one who had helped her find work in the security organs. Which had also come about by chance. A certain very handsome man used to visit this woman to comfort her during her husband's long drinking binges and other absences. He didn't wear a uniform, but he carried a work-issue gun with him at all times. And this woman was happy to be helpful in other ways too. One time the man told her about a well-paid vacancy, obviously hoping that she would apply; unfortunately she couldn't type, but she knew that Lidia could turn her hand to that kind of work. Later, when it turned out that this man was only interested in getting information about her husband's colleagues, they fell out badly. After that another man started to come round and console her. He was no less handsome, but he had completely different views, he was one of the leading figures among the local Russian nationalists. Lidia's former neighbour was happy to be helpful to him in every way possible too. And this nationalist really liked those plump women with pale skin and a slightly motherly appearance, so they were well suited to each other. You might not believe it but back in those days the Estonian and Russian nationalists got on marvellously, united as they were by a common hatred for the Bolshevik regime – although the Estonians believed that the Soviet occupation which started in 1940 was a much worse crime than the execution of the last Russian tsar and his family, as ugly as that might have been. At the necessary moments they'd helped each other out of trouble before. Moreover, the Russian nationalists thought that if copies of KGB files made it through to the West, then it would be a great help for their cause too.

In addition to Lidia Petrovna's name, two other names reached Valev's organisation in the same way, but it proved impossible to make an approach to them. And the fact that Lidia Petrovna had once worked at Raim's school was certainly going to be useful.

Valev knew nothing more about her. And that was for the best.

At the precise moment that Lidia opened the door of her apartment – dressed in her dressing gown and feeling some trepidation, since her doorbell rarely rang – Raim had still not thought up the words with which to address his former Russian teacher after all those years.

But when he saw the immediate, complete and unambiguous look of recognition in her eyes, he realised that sometimes it was not necessary to think – only to be.

He closed the door behind him, put the cake and flowers on top of the cupboard in the corridor, took hold of Lidia's shoulders, pulled her gently towards him, slid his hands under her dressing gown, across her naked back, and pressed his lips on to hers.

In other words, he did exactly what he'd always wanted to do every single time he'd seen Lidia Petrovna.

Who cares about cake when there are fingers, hair, a nose, lips, a hollow in the back, shoulder blades, buttocks, and breasts? Who cares about flowers when a warm, moist welcome beckons from between the legs, and trousers can no longer contain the urge which has been suppressed for all those long years? Fortunately Lidia managed to edge slowly backwards, guiding them into the bedroom, so that they could become one for the first time on her quilt rather than on the corridor floor. But could anyone rightfully demand greater self-restraint when every square centimetre of their flesh yearned to be pressed against the long-awaited other, pressed so firmly that it could never be prised loose? Can you ask why someone who is parched after weeks in the desert drinks so greedily that the water sloshes out from either side of the jug?

If only he'd thought to come here before, and not for the reason which had eventually brought him.

In the town which Lidia Petrovna originally came from, wherever it was (Voronezh, Suzdal, Irkutsk, some other Russian town, Raim couldn't remember exactly), they believed that the vocation of Russian teacher was well suited to a pretty, decent girl who had the good sense and motivation to take seriously her studies at the local peda-gogical institute. All the more so that with her looks there was slim chance she would be one of those long-serving teachers who end up as shrewish old maids. They taught her how she was supposed to understand those obscure poems, and she even got to stand in front of a class a bit before getting herself fixed up with a man and leaving. Naturally, her love and respect for the great language of Pushkin, Turgenev and Mayakovsky did not go anywhere. And wherever she lived they would beckon her out from the four walls of domesticity to go and follow her vocation. After all, there were schools everywhere, and a shortage of good Russian teachers – here in Estonia too. How could she have known that by choosing to come and live in this coun-try she was getting herself caught up in someone's grand project, a project which aimed to deprive all those clumsy, lanky boys and precocious plaited-hair girls, together with their parents, uncles, aunts, neighbours, relatives and their colleagues of that strange, incomprehensible language which they spoke amongst themselves? But gradually she started to realise that something was not quite right. It was evident from the way some of them started looking at her in the classroom or corridor, as if she were a guest who had outstayed her welcome. It was evident from the way in which the other teachers suddenly stopped talking when she entered the staffroom. Why didn't they realise that she was not the problem? She wanted to explain, but somehow she couldn't get her mouth round that strange and incom-prehensible language; it was as if it just didn't want to give up the sounds it was used to. So she preferred to stick to her wonderful mother tongue, which she spoke beautifully, and she knew that they understood, so it was easier for everyone that way. But some things remained unsaid of course. Over time she got used to the situation, just like everyone else. She comforted herself with the thought that Pushkin, Turgenev and Mayakovsky would stay who they were regardless of what was said in their beautiful language in sepulchral tones on the nine o'clock news on television every night. She didn't know that not a single one of those lanky boys or plaited-hair girls, nor the women who fell silent when she entered the staffroom, ever watched those news programmes. She took pride when one of her students occasionally saw themselves reflected in the heroes and heroines of Russian literature and she saw a spark of comprehension in their eyes which spanned the gap between two worlds. The chance of that happening made her life worth living. And at home she had her books. She went to the ballet, and sometimes the opera. And to concerts. Occasionally the cinema. There wasn't much else.

And the situation remained the same when she left her position at the school. She used to shrug off any doubts about the nature of her new work; she didn't have anything to hide. Anyway, the salary was nearly two times bigger, the hours significantly shorter, and she didn't have to wear a uniform. She quickly got used to leaving gaps in the right places, and she was quite happy that she was not authorised to know what the papers were about. It was other peoples' business to fill them in.

But sometimes things take many years to reach their culmination, and if the outcome is a good one, then why not be happy?

Raim was in the eleventh grade back then. He was standing in front of the class, and Lidia Petrovna was saying nothing. Strictly speaking, Raim had been caught out, but there was something about him which resembled a budding exhibitionist who was savouring being completely naked for the first time.

Raim was good at drawing, especially pictures of things which were important to him. He'd gone to art class for six years before his father decided that it was better to be good at one thing than mediocre at many, and so Raim had chosen volleyball – there was no other way, he was already captain of the team by then. But of course he kept on doodling away for his own pleasure. And the picture which he had accidently left in between the pages of his Russian exercise book was a really good one. An Art Institute lecturer wouldn't have expected anything better from one of their student's life drawings – except this picture was not drawn from real life but from imagination, from desire, from adoration.

Lidia Petrovna was lost for words. She raised her eyes and looked at this boy – to be honest he was virtually a man already – who had seen her like that in his mind's eye. It was clear that the picture had been drawn from the purest and truest of motivations. Of course she knew where to draw the line of propriety, but she couldn't restrain a fleeting thought which sent a shudder right through to the tips of her toes.

She knew very well that she would have to handle the situation like a normal person. Not like a teacher. If she wanted to remain a normal person, that is. Because she would still be a teacher whatever she did.

"Sit down," she said with a slightly hoarse voice, and gave the exercise book back to Raim. That was it. She kept the picture, and never raised the subject again.

But Raim would have been happy to know that the very same evening Lidia Petrovna stood naked in front of her mirror for a while, looking at herself. And for the first time in ages she liked what she saw.

In fact Raim had come to Lidia Petrovna's block two days earlier, but without going in. He remembered the address from his school days; one evening he'd followed her all the way to her front door, without her even knowing. It was strange, but after all those years he still mentally referred to her by her first name and patronymic, Russian style. He'd just got used to it. Of course the other students had called her Lidia Petrovna too, because that was required as a sign of respect, but when her back was turned everyone knew her simply as Gromova, and that was who she remained, since not a single nickname stuck. Everyone apart from Raim that is, who knew her as Lidia Petrovna, even in his thoughts.

Raim wasn't sure that his former teacher would still be living there, but Lidia Petrovna was very happy in her small Pelgulinna flat. She had moved there after separating from her husband, part-exchanging it for her three-room Mustamäe apartment, which had left her with enough money to decorate properly and even to buy herself the occasional dress to go to the opera in – so that the men who saw her wouldn't think she was one of those culture widows. Maybe her new place wasn't as comfortable as the old one, but she couldn't stand the sympathetic looks of her husband's former colleagues who lived in her old block. And she'd got used to the new place by now.

And now, it should be added, she certainly didn't want to move anywhere else.

Raim had stood on the other side of the street, trying as hard as he could to think up what he would say on the off chance that Lidia Petrovna's flat was not occupied by new inhabitants who might have her forwarding address.

But when Lidia Petrovna appeared at the front door he recognised her straight away. Fortunately she didn't glance in Raim's direction but headed straight off towards town. Beautiful, majestic and completely her own woman, just as if all those years had never passed.

"I've been living here for ages," said Lidia Petrovna, "and you only just found me."

It was actually a question, but Raim didn't yet know how to answer.

"I still have that drawing of yours somewhere," Lidia Petrovna said with a grin.

The Lenbumprom delegation travelled back by air, since Gennady Vassilyevich had to be sure to return in time for his son-in-law's birthday party that evening. As soon as they arrived back at Pulkovo Airport he said goodbye to the rest of the group and headed straight for the VIP channel; if they'd gone by train he would have had to wait with the others while customs went through everyone's bag. The procedure always took more time coming back from Finland.

Alex collected his small suitcase from the luggage carousel and headed for the customs queue. Unfortunately a large number of passengers from Finnair's New York flight had transferred on to their flight, and they had trolley-loads of cases and bags with them, so it looked like they had a long wait ahead. Alex was tired and sweaty, and by now the effects of the wine he'd drunk during the pre-departure lunch were starting to wear off, which wasn't a particularly pleasant sensation. He wasn't afraid of anything happening at customs, since he had hardly anything of any interest with him apart from a couple of Miles Davis albums. He noted with a sigh that the other queue, which the majority of the Leningrad Paper Industry people had decided to join, was now moving slightly faster, but there was no point in changing queues.

The customs desk gradually got closer and closer, until finally the rather elderly Jewish man who was standing in front of Alex started to lift his cases with New York luggage tags one by one on to the conveyor. First the big ones, then the smaller ones, and then the duty-free carrier bags at the very end. The old man was sweating a lot more than Alex.

There were two customs officials: one to look at the contents of the cases on a screen, the other to rummage about in the cases which had been opened.

"Do you fancy a beer?" the second customs official asked his colleague when the duty-free bag had finally come out of the other end of the X-ray machine. The old man was

74

standing there holding his passport and customs declaration in one hand, and trying to work out whether he was now allowed to put his things back on to the trolley.

"See what he's got," the first customs official said, without lifting his gaze from the screen in front of him.

The duty-free bag had come from a shop at Helsinki Airport.

"Nikolay," the second customs official said, yanking himself a can from the six-pack and opening it.

"Ah, I'm not so keen on Nikolay, it always gives me a headache," the first one said.

"Excuse me," the bag's owner said in Russian which had a heavy Odessa accent, "is bringing beer into the Soviet Union banned now?" He was still holding his passport and the customs declaration in his hand.

"Hey, no one was talking to you," the second customs official said in his direction, taking a long swig from the can.

"I was just asking," the old man said in a fluster. "But how about a stamp, do I get a stamp in my papers now?"

"Ah, he was just asking," the customs official sneered. "Maybe he thinks he's got rights or something?"

"He's an émigré now this one," the other one sniggered from behind the screen.

"We're still dealing with you," the customs official informed the man, pointing at the largest of his suitcases. "Show us what's in this one!"

With shaking hands the man turned the case on its side and snapped the lock open. Inside were neatly packed dress shirts, a stripy wool jumper and a large teddy bear with a pink ribbon around its neck. The customs official pulled it out of the case.

"Hey, Vasya, we had some sort of tip-off about drugs hidden in soft toys, didn't we?" he shouted over to the first official, without taking his gaze off the man.

"We sure did," the other one laughed.

"Now then," the official announced, placing his beer

on the conveyor belt and taking a pair of scissors from the drawer. "Will you cut it open yourself, or should I?"

"Please, comrades, stop it, take all my beers instead, that bear is a present for my granddaughter!" said the old man in alarm, but the customs official had already stabbed the bear in the stomach with the scissors, sending filling material flying in all directions. The official then made a show of rummaging about inside the bear's stomach for a bit before throwing it back to the man.

"Please accept my apologies on behalf of the Soviet Customs Committee," announced the official with a broad smile. "There was a mistake, you can go now." He picked up the stamp and marked the man's customs declaration.

"That's just incredible!" said the old man, unable to restrain himself any longer. "You're some kind of ... I don't know what..."

"Yes Comrade Citizen, I'm listening..." said the customs official. "Maybe we should do a full body search on this one?" he added to his colleague.

"No, leave the fucker alone, Sanyok," grunted the man behind the screen. "I'm not struck on poking around his fat arse."

By now the people in the queue had grown more and more edgy, and a woman standing behind Alex had furtively fished a twenty-mark note out of her pocket and placed it between the pages of her passport.

"Gather up your bits and bobs old man," said the customs official in an almost friendly tone. "The homeland awaits."

"And what exactly are you looking at?" the other official asked Alex coldly.

"Nothing," Alex said in a similarly flat tone, and he placed his suitcase on the conveyor.

"Please tell me the grounds on which I am being detained," Karl demanded. "And whether I am entitled to see a lawyer."

He was making a point of behaving calmly and politely, but he looked quite different to the last time he'd been sitting on that stool by Särg's table. He had a large bruise under his left eye, his right brow was badly messed up and his knuckles were bloody. Arrangements had been made so that Karl was not held in the investigation cell with everyone else, where information could leak out, but in a separate room, which also happened to house two alcoholic ex-boxers.

"You see, even a petty Soviet criminal can't stand a suspected traitor," Särg said.

"How did you reach that conclusion?" Karl asked. "I dropped the soap and slipped over."

"Do you want medical treatment?"

Karl shrugged.

"Not yet," he mumbled. "But I would like to see a lawyer, like I said."

Särg leant across the table in Karl's direction. He knew that Fyodor Kuzmich demanded results; he also knew that they wouldn't get any today, if at all, but he had to work with what he was given.

"You yourself claim that the Soviet Union is not a law-based state, isn't that so?" he said quietly, looking Karl directly in the eyes. "So then, we'll let you spend some time in the version of the Soviet Union in which you and your friends believe. To start with, you are aware that there is no paperwork to prove that you are here at all? On the one hand that gives us more options. But then it gives you more too. If we come to an agreement then you'll get a genuine medical note to take to work to say that you have been in hospital all this time, that you were taken there unconscious following a car accident. What do you reckon?"

It seemed that Karl hadn't been listening to what Särg said at all.

"Now I remember where I have seen you before," he said.

It's nice when a person has something other than work and family in his life. For Särg this was his stamp collection.

He first got involved in this hobby some years earlier, and quite by chance. An international criminal network had been using rare postage stamps to move money across the border. The stamps were almost impossible to discover in customs checks, but it was subsequently not too difficult to turn them back into money using well-established channels. Since Särg was known for being the best amongst his colleagues at memorising large amounts of information, and for actually enjoying it too, he was given the assignment of infiltrating the stamp-collecting community. The first thing that came to Särg's mind was a crime novel by the Polish writer Andrzej Piwowarczyk, which he'd read several times at university, called *The Open Window*, in which one captain Gleb chased a criminal who was operating amongst a group of philatelists. The very first time he read the book Särg had felt an urge to start a stamp album, but he couldn't allow himself such an expensive hobby while he was studying. Things were different now though: the security services allocated him some money for the purpose, and he was also given a couple of confiscated stamp collections to use. He was able to put together a few items from these collections to start his own, which meant that he would be taken seriously at the club which met at the Teacher's House and among those men who gathered under the arch beside the stamp shop at the Pärnu road end of Lauristin Street (now Roosikrantsi Street). From then on Särg seriously caught the stamp-collecting bug. The first things he made sure to get were the *Zumstein* and *Yvert et Tellier* catalogues which were gathering dust in the windows of the second-hand bookshop on Mündi Street so that he could establish the overall value of his collection. Then he bought a number of full series from the stamp club – a couple of rarer items with pictures of President Konstantin Päts, some with a mail pigeon on them, and some Soviet stamps bearing a Pernau postal mark, which stayed in circulation for a short time during the German occupation, before the "Estland/Eesti" series was issued. They cost a fair bit, since people hadn't managed to send many letters in that short period of time, so the stamps were obviously rarer and more sought after. Some time later, when he and his collection were already better known in stamp-collecting circles, he would slip it into conversations that he could arrange the sale of some Elva stamps to anyone who might be interested, since he'd been offered them but wasn't keen. These were the rarest stamps in Estonian postal history, some of them worth thousands of dollars. It was likely that the people he was trying to track down would be interested in precisely those kinds of stamps. But much to his superiors' surprise, Särg refused to interrogate the criminals once they were caught, justifying this by his desire to protect his reputation in the stamp-collecting world. Who knew when his connections there might become useful again? There were a lot of murky goings-on in the stamp business. His superiors could see his point. Naturally he had to hand over the collection which had been bought with KGB money, but by then his own personal collection was actually better than that one, and so he carried on going to the Teachers' House on Sundays before meeting Galina in front of Sõprus cinema.

As for Karl, he had a pretty decent collection of sports-themed stamps. Nothing exceptional, but all the same.

"You shouldn't let them beat him up like that, Comrade Major," said Särg. "It doesn't produce any results."

"I make the decisions around here," Vinkel snorted. He actually agreed, but that didn't mean he would let his subordinates tell him what to do. What's more he was hungry, and his bosses had demanded a report from him, but he didn't have any good news for them.

"In that case I ask for your permission to return to the sixth department," Särg requested. "I've got a lot of work on with my own cases anyway, and it's looking pretty clear by now that this case doesn't have anything to do with economic crime."

"Expressing our views, are we Comrade Captain?" Vinkel said with a wink. "You can actually be quite sure that you'll soon be very interested in this particular case."

Särg didn't understand what was meant by that. Unlike us, dear reader, because we have reason to suspect that this Anton – the one who didn't return to the cellar from the picket with the others but went straight home – and Captain Särg's son, the history buff and self-proclaimed true Estonian, are one and the same person. And from that it is easy to draw conclusions about the company which Anton Särg kept and who his friends were, and then to conjecture that it was very probable Anton Särg would eventually end up in one of the pictures taken by those plain-clothed policemen with their long-focus lenses as they sat and observed the insurrectionary youth.

Anton could not shake the fear that he would never be fully accepted as one of the gang, even when they started giving him tasks which involved a high level of responsibility. He was terribly ashamed of his slight Russian accent and occasional slip-ups with the partitive plural, even if all the rest of them were completely used to it and took it as nothing more than a personal quirk. It never occurred to anyone to call him a bloody Russky.

But this is how it had happened:

The history teacher, Comrade Kovalyova, had been ill the day when she was supposed to teach an extra lesson on the subject of the Molotov-Ribbentrop Pact and explain that the information spread by Western propaganda radio stations regarding some sort of secret protocol hadn't been corroborated; Soviet historians had searched the archives for the document, but since it did not exist, it could not be found. Moreover, at the moment when Nazi Germany and the Soviet Union signed the non-aggression treaty it had been a necessary step, giving the leadership breathing room to prepare for the test of strength which was soon to ensue. And it was highly regrettable that so many people had allowed themselves to be misled, organising the so-called Baltic Chain and demanding the abrogation of something which didn't even exist in the first place.

It was that cold, dark time of year, teacher Kovalyova was already getting on in years, and she was not in the best of health, so there was nothing surprising about her falling ill. But that lesson couldn't just be cancelled: the order had come from above and it had to be executed.

So teacher Kovalyova had to give that lesson a week later, on the day on which Estonians celebrated Christmas.

The extra history class took place straight after the other lessons were finished. Teacher Kovalyova had been in front of a class of students since morning and was already really tired, but as far as she was concerned she managed to deliver her text pretty enthusiastically and convincingly.

"Are there any questions?" she asked. "Would anyone like any points clarified?"

One hand went up. It was Class 9b's top student, Anton Särg.

"Go on, Anton," said teacher Kovalyova.

"There is one thing I would like clarifying," said Anton, standing up. "If it is really true, as you say, that this additional protocol never existed, then why is it that the Soviet Congress of People's Deputies declared it null and void today, with effect from the moment it was signed."

Deportations.
A war of independence – not the Civil War.
Mass murder in Tartu's prisons.
And of course the Gulag.

Now try saying something without lying for a change.
Or just fuck off.

Maarja and Raim were on the third floor of the Pegasus café. It was nice and quiet here during the day, just the odd hung-over poet coming up the stairs to check if there was anyone he knew, but there wasn't. On a hot day like this it would have made more sense to be outside, Maarja thought. Looking out of the large windows towards the other side of the street, at the mounds outside Niguliste church, she could see ten or so smallish groups who had taken a seat, each with a plastic bag of goodies. But it was definitely more private here inside, that was true.

Maarja had been unsure until the very last moment whether she would return to the picket. She couldn't even say why she had put money into the collection jar. Naturally she wanted the same things as everyone else: she'd taken part in the unofficial singing nights and signed up for the Estonian Citizens' Committee long ago, and during the congress of the Popular Front she had sat with her parents, glued to the radio from morning to evening. But she had yet to decide for herself whether it was a good thing that there were so many of those activists groups. On the one hand it could mean that one of them was bound to get lucky. But it could also mean that they would blow so much hot air fighting amongst themselves that the important things would simply be forgotten. So it was a little strange to find herself sitting there drinking cheap red wine with this guy who didn't have any doubts of that kind.

Otherwise, though, he was quite all right, even very much so. And he radiated some kind of power, some sort of certainty, so you were sure right away that you could rely on him, that he knew how things were. Not that Maarja found him attractive as such: despite all their inner confidence those blond, broad-shouldered types were a bit ordinary – not stupid or anything, ordinary in the right way, just like straight-talking and clean water. Transparent, yes, that was the right word. Not that he didn't have any secrets, everyone had them, just that those secrets were somehow clear.

It is true that it's impossible to live without clean water, but clean water is not enough on its own.

In any case it was pretty cool to be drinking wine with him. Anyway the other girls were either at work, in the countryside, or elsewhere.

"May you live in interesting times"

In 1936, shortly before Sir Hughe Montgomery Knatchbull-Hugessen departed on a diplomatic mission to China, one of his friends told him about a Chinese curse he had once heard: "May you live in interesting times!" Or at least that is what Knatchbull-Hugessen claims in his memoires. There are some other British authors who appear to have known of such an expression too. The Chinese, however, do not. The closest thing in meaning which they have is the following: "It is better to live as a dog in peaceful times than as a human in a world of confusion."

And what about it?

Just like anyone else, I have done things in my life which I am not proud of, and even one or two things which I regret. But I have no reason to be anything other than happy that I have lived in the period when I have, and that I have been able to experience one world changing into another. So what if this has stirred hungers in me which have damaged me? I am willing to pay that price, if only for the perspective it gave me, which is something I do not encounter in people who have lived under only one political order.

You have to find someone who no one could ever, ever, link with you and your group, Valev had said. But in whom you can place absolute trust. That means less risk for that person, and more importantly, less risk for our cause. If it's a schoolmate, relative, work brigade member, and they end up getting caught for some reason, then even if they keep their lips sealed you will have the security services at your door in half an hour flat.

It's easy for him to talk, Raim thought, but just try telling this girl that she now has to go and put everything on the line in the name of Estonian independence.

"What's up?" Maarja asked, and she laughed her ringing laugh. "You've got an expression on your face like you're about to make me a marriage proposal."

"So you get them often then?" Raim asked, and he laughed too.

"Well at least a couple of times a week," Maarja replied trying to keep a straight face, but not succeeding particularly well.

When Alex got to work in the morning Konstantin Zakharovich gave him a slightly odd look before informing him that Gennady Vassilyevich was waiting for him in his office. Which meant he had to go and see him right away. Gennady Vassilyevich started by inquiring, with contrived joviality, how Alex was, and then told him that he would have to drop by the city administration, since the mayor's foreign affairs advisor, one Vladimir Vladimirovich, apparently wanted to see him.

Even after I put the final full stop in the draft of this story, it took me a long time to shake the moods which it evoked in me. It was hard to think of anything else. The story itself has changed quite a lot in the meantime, but the most important details have stayed the same. And I still feel that I am somehow trapped inside it. Although I am simultaneously unburdened of the parts of myself which I left there, and I feel that I can now write what I want – or even nothing at all.

The first time I saw it was in a dream. Or at least, part of it, Maarja and Alex's story, which we will get to soon. It was just like a film, in fact it really was a film which I was watching while I slept. But it took place in Poland. The café where they met was right inside the art museum there, not like the café in Kadriorg. But the museum was just like our one. I still remember the chinking of Maarja's spoon against the plate as she ate her cake. So some memories never fade. It was summer in my dream and in real life, the sun was scorching hot and I could hear the gentle murmur of the sea.

Without fully realising why, Alex sensed that this couldn't mean anything good, since good news would normally just land on your desk in the course of other business, for no apparent reason. Good news was not something which you as an individual, specifically you, whoever you happened to be, would have earned, and where your role would have to be specifically emphasised. No, good news just happened by chance, since the reasons why the system might suddenly smile upon you would be random and unknowable, and had to remain that way. Bad news was something altogether different. It could involve you having to personally account for some misfortune which you had no way at all of preventing. Like, for example, when the father of one of Alex's classmates oversaw the building of a children's home which then burnt down, and this happened to be the same children's home which the second secretary of the Communist Party's regional office had personally opened on TV. It burnt down because the building brigade foreman had used up all the insulation materials which met the required fire safety standards to build a country cottage for his direct superior, the deputy director of the trust. But the system reacted swiftly and mercilessly against the father of Alex's classmate, because it was his signature which was on the documentation signing off the building for use, there for everyone to see. Rights and responsibilities are not in fact equally balanced. You can easily end up being responsible without having any rights at all.

In other words, if Vladimir Vladimirovich wanted to see Alex personally, it couldn't mean good news. In the world of good news, Alex simply did not exist for Vladimir Vladimirovich.

The Smolny Institute was originally established at some point in the beginning of the nineteenth century for the education of aristocratic young ladies. A hundred years or so later it housed Lenin's headquarters and apartment, from where he oversaw the processes which engulfed the whole of the Russian Empire following the October Revolution. Now there were no longer any orders flying out from this building across the world, but the lifeblood of Leningrad and the surrounding region still flowed from here. Alex had never been to the Smolny before, but he could roughly imagine what it would be like: wide staircases, red carpets, high-ceilinged offices big enough to ride a bike through, probably built as classrooms originally, but now every important official had one to himself. And there to guard the peace would be reliable, bulldog-faced ladies over forty, who had no idea whatsoever what life without constant constipation could be like.

Alex turned out to be a bit off-mark regarding those ladies. The woman sitting in Vladimir Vladimirovich's outer office was no more than a couple of years older than him, she was elegant, stylishly dressed and wore glasses, and turned out to be friendly too. She offered him tea and told him he only had three-quarters of an hour to wait. Some sort of changes were clearly afoot.

When Alex entered the office he breathed a sigh of relief. Vladimir Vladimirovich, a short fisheyed man, was sitting at his desk the other end of the office, but Alex had good eyesight so he could see what was there straight away – the latest issue of the Finnish weekly *Suomen Kuvalehti*, open at the pages containing Alex's interview with Silja; Alex's picture was on the left-hand page, and there was a picture of Alex's uncle on the right. In other words, nothing too damning.

"Now then," said Vladimir Vladimirovich. "This here. Your doing, if I'm not mistaken?"

"Yes," said Alex with a nod.

"Don'tinterruptmewhenI'mtalking,"VladimirVladimirovich continued. "You are aware that Olga Anatolyevna coordinates public relations for your department?"

"Yes, I am," said Alex with a nod.

"So why did Olga Anatolyevna not know anything about your interview? Eh?"

"I was planning…" Alex started to say.

"Listen, will you let me speak or not?" Vladimir Vladimirovich glared at Alex just long enough for him to start to feel that he was expecting an answer, but Alex said nothing just in case. "Anyway, make sure you don't do anything like this again."

Alex noticed a very handsome gold Swiss watch on Vladimir Vladimirovich's wrist.

"I'm sorry," said Alex, "but I didn't say anything out of line."

Vladimir Vladimirovich gave a weary sigh.

"You don't need me to explain anything further, I hope," he said, picking up the newspaper and starting to leaf through it, almost as if he were seeking confirmation for what he'd just said. He'd already turned the pages five or six times when he next looked up from the table.

"You're still here?"

Alex had got the message.

But this is what happened next: the very moment when Alex closed the door of Vladimir Vladimirovich's office behind him and felt his secretary's sympathetic gaze on him, he for some reason recalled a feeling which he had last felt a very long time ago, during his first year at university. It was a feeling of yearning for another place, which he and his friends had once given a specific name. Back in those days the Marlboro-puffing Komsomol creeps got on everyone's nerves. They would pepper their official speeches with Lenin and Brezhnev quotations without bothering to think about what they actually meant, and they would turn up at the parties organised by the prettiest girls in the student halls and tell filthy jokes, although they would be sure to keep their ties on at all times. Something just wasn't quite right about it. The realities of student life didn't help things much: in the autumn the students were taken out to the collective farm to dig potatoes for a month in place of their studies. They did a little work, but the ground was always cold and the tractor driver always drunk, so there wasn't much left for it but to hit the vodka. Sometimes they were instructed to go to the vegetable warehouse on a Sunday, where they would be asked to sort through filthy boxes full of frozen, rotten crap, with scant chance of finding anything edible. And so, as unbelievable as it may now sound, they decided that the place they yearned for was North Korea. Because things must be different there. There, the students got up at five every morning of their own accord so as to have time to go and work in the factory for a couple of hours before lectures, and no one would feel any need for fancy clothes and Marlboros. You get my point. Back then they were sure that the same spirit must still exist somewhere in the Soviet Union, it had to. That ardour which had helped the Bolsheviks to beat the White Guards during the Russian Civil War, that belief in the cause.

Now that same feeling, that same long-forgotten childish feeling reared into Alex's conscience one again. Only to immediately shatter into little pieces, like a window smashed with a stone. Let's be honest, it was long overdue.

We see them at the moment when the same thought passes through both their minds: what if our marriage is over? Come to an end? Raim's father is in the loo, he has just tugged his flies closed but not yet flushed the toilet, and he has coughed up the phlegm accumulated in his throat and spat it out. They've got a Polish toilet bowl, with a flush button on the side of the cistern, not a cord hanging from ceiling height. Meanwhile his wife, who expects him to be absent from the room for a while, has swiftly opened the drinks cabinet door, taken out a bottle of Kirsberry Danish liqueur and a glass, and started pouring herself a drink. The large glob of spit and phlegm strikes the surface of the water at exactly the moment when the stream of sweet sticky liquid reaches the bottom of the glass, and that is the very same moment when, completely independently of each other, they both think exactly the same thought: what if it is over, what if it really is? What next? Not that either of them had done anything wrong exactly, no, they strictly adhered to all the moral norms, or at least their understanding of those norms. But without some minor, petty breaking of the laws, rules and conventions, it was impossible to survive in a society which was organised so that every single person felt a little bit guilty before the state – which itself was completely pure and holy. After all, only humans make mistakes, the system was flawless. But let's not stray from the subject. Raim's mother blames herself for secretly having been a little too proud of her son. She'd already seen a perfect little man in him from that time at Grandfather's funeral when, barely five, he was all dressed up in a black suit. It had seemed to come naturally to him to take up his place at the end of the row of people receiving the condolence messages and endure there for a whole hour and a half, looking serious and dignified as he shook every last guest's hand. She remembered that image the clearest of all from her father-in-law's funeral – not the journey to Pärnamäe, not the graveside speeches, nor the hysterical biddy and her dim daughter, whose existence they'd known nothing about while her father-in-law was still alive. No, she remembered her grown-up little boy most of all. He still caused a slight sense of unease which she couldn't properly describe; she still wanted to poke her head round his door every evening and wave him goodnight, but it just wasn't appropriate any more. Her tough little boy. But maybe she shouldn't have made so many assumptions. A person can't be shiny and indestructible like a precious stone – and even some of those can be quite opaque. But once you have got used to thinking of them as strong, then it doesn't occur to you that they may also have their weaknesses, and may occasionally need your help. Raim's mother did not know what her son's weaknesses were, but something clearly wasn't right if he didn't come home at night any more. It's not that he simply didn't turn up, leaving her waiting until morning, sitting in the kitchen tugging on a cigarette; he would phone in the evening and inform them that he wasn't coming home, but with no further explanation. You're not going to say: What do you mean you're not coming? We're having cheesecake for pudding and the latest episode of *Hercule Poirot* is showing on Finnish television. Because if he still doesn't come, then it must be your fault, you must have been doing something wrong all along, why else would he rather be somewhere else? Raim's father asks himself the same question, although from a different perspective: Maybe I should have been stricter with him, demanded more of him? You should always ask more of someone who is capable. Meanwhile he is waiting to hear the plopping sound at any moment, because the glob of spit and phlegm has already reached the surface of the water; technically the process which will produce the plop has already begun, it's just that the air vibrations have not yet transmitted that information to his ears. Maybe I should have insisted on a regime of early rising and workouts; that would have been good for me as well. We went running in the forest now and again in the summer, he liked that; we did squats and press-ups by the tree felled by the storm. Maybe I should have thought something up for winter as well, like cold showers to toughen the constitution, and I could have fixed a bar in the doorway to do chin-ups. Although to hell with cold water, the main thing is discipline, order, respect for one's parents. It's just not on, phoning like that and saying you're not coming home, without a word of explanation about where you are or what you're doing. What kind of home is it if you can just decide not to come back like that? What kind of family? No kind of family at all. Hell. Damn it. I toil like a draught horse and that's the thanks I get. And then, a millisecond or so later, the plopping sound reaches his ears, he presses the flush and the water washes everything away. But what it leaves behind, his world, is just the same as before. Raim's parents don't yet know it, but in less than ten years Estonian television will start to show home-grown serials depicting everyday life, and the scriptwriters will try to create characters just like them for the viewers to have a well-meaning laugh at. And Raim's parents will laugh too, because they won't recognise themselves in those characters. And that is for the best.

"What a total bastard you are!" said Lidia Petrovna, trying to hide the tremor in her voice.

She was sitting up in bed and smoking, with her satin pyjama jacket open. Raim had just placed the Minox EC camera on the bedside cupboard and explained to Lidia Petrovna how to use it, and what kinds of pictures she should take with it.

For Raim the moment which followed seemed to last much longer than it actually did, because he had little experience of such situations.

But Lidia Petrovna now had two options.

Her employers would assume that she would inform them about the conversation which had just taken place, and as a consequence Raim would then be arrested, most probably followed by several of his friends and acquaintances, especially the acquaintance who had given Raim that wonderful piece of equipment invented by the Baltic German engineer. In other words, her employers would have assumed that she would betray her lover.

Her lover, however, assumed that she would put her liberty and maybe even her life on the line to join a struggle that she didn't necessarily identify with in order to enable something to pass across the border between two worlds, something which might eventually determine the fate of many people, most of whom she didn't even know. In other words, that she would betray her employers.

The question was which of those scenarios would result in Lidia Petrovna betraying herself.

In other words, there was no question.

In those days there was no ferry crossing between Tallinn and Stockholm. Ordinary people got there first by taking the Georg Ots ferry to Finland, staying the night with some friends, meeting up with some other friends the next day and then boarding the evening Silja Line ferry. You didn't need to book a cabin as there was the so-called *sleep-in* option, which entitled you to make use of an oblong patch marked on the floor and a mattress placed there for the purpose. The next morning you would alight in the Kingdom of Sweden. However, having being found guilty of anti-Soviet activities and punished by being expelled from the country, Ervin arrived in Sweden by plane, flying on the Moscow-Copenhagen-Stockholm-Bangkok route. Such a route really did exist, and the tickets were relatively cheap too. So Ervin got his first experience of the free world in Copenhagen airport, having had to disembark with his escort while the plane refuelled. The escort was a Russian man of few words; Ervin was unsure if he was fully aware of Ervin's role in the larger scheme of things, and he obviously didn't choose to tell him about it. He had no money with him, just the twenty kilos of personal possessions which he had checked in.

Ervin was met at the airport in Stockholm by pleasant old dears in floppy hats holding a basketful of bananas for him and a sign with his photo and the words "Welcome to Freedom!" on it. That was a lofty phrase. Ervin nodded goodbye to his escort, who was met by a car from the Soviet Embassy, and then left with the old ladies.

"To start with we're going to the Estonian House," the women chirped, "you'll get a light meal there and meet some people, Tiit and Jüri are already waiting. You'll have an interview with our newspaper, the *Estonian Daily*, about the latest developments in the liberation struggle in occupied Estonia. Tonight you'll be staying at Medborgarplatsen: Konrad Muld has promised to put you up to start with, he has a spare guest room, and he's a single gentleman like you. But you'll get something better pretty soon, when all the paperwork is in order, don't you worry, it's not like Russia here, the government actually functions."

It turned out to be a tiring day, with nothing more than fruit juice and coffee to drink. That evening Ervin discovered to his disappointment that, to put it delicately, Konrad Muld lived up to his surname; it meant soil in Estonian, and he really was as old as the proverbial soil. He clearly had some difficulty getting round his apartment, and he constantly had a worried demeanour. Having shown Ervin the cupboard where the sheets and blankets were kept, he went into the other room to watch the news on TV. But once Ervin had finished making his bed he poked his head around the door, and Mr Muld switched off the television and offered him a cup of tea.

"Do you get the feeling," he started to ask in a wavering voice, "that recent events indicate that Communist rule in Estonia may finally be coming to an end?"

"I certainly do," Ervin answered, and smiled at the thought that it was possible to say that out loud without having to look around in case anyone heard.

"Well I won't live to see it," said Konrad with a sigh. "But I would like to see my granddaughters again."

"Are they in Estonia then?" Ervin asked.

"Where else, yes," Konrad replied, and stood up again. "Wait, I'll show you a picture." The bookshelf was full of photo albums.

"Maybe some other time," Ervin said. "It's been a pretty long day."

"As you wish," Konrad concurred. "Now then, don't be offended, but maybe I could help you out with a bit of money?"

"That would be very kind," Ervin said with a nod. "Maybe we could also have a little drop of something to mark our getting acquainted?"

"Oh yes," said Konrad with a nod. "I don't drink myself any more, but I always have something in for guests."

He went to the kitchen and after searching for a while came back with a bottle which was a third full of sweet blackcurrant liqueur.

The next morning Konrad woke Ervin at ten so that he could get to Norrmalmstorget by twelve. It had been agreed that he would speak at the demonstrations which took place every Monday, and it was quite possible that someone from the Swedish Foreign Ministry would come to meet the latest person to be expelled. Unfortunately the breakfast at Konrad's was meagre, consisting of weak instant coffee, sandwiches made with some kind of strong-tasting cheese, and a hard-boiled egg. Ervin hoped that someone would invite him to eat after the demonstration.

There turned out to be a lot of people at Norrmalmstorget and some familiar faces from back home caught Ervin's eye – poets, probably. Damn, thought Ervin, worrying that they would grab all the attention, but it turned out that he didn't need to worry, for as soon as people discovered who he was, journalists and activists flocked around him, a couple of important-looking men shook his hand, and someone whispered in his ear that they were Gunnar Hökmark and Håkan Holmberg, although those names meant nothing to Ervin. English wasn't one of his strong points, but the younger Estonians there were happy to help interpret and he didn't object, since he assumed (not without reason) that he sounded cleverer in translation. After all, he wasn't to blame that the occupying regime hadn't let him get a decent education.

There were two men watching all of this from a distance: one of them a lanky guy with glasses, the other a chubby chap with a moustache. Straight out of a comedy film. "The vultures are circling," someone next to Ervin said, pointing them out. Ervin didn't understand at first. "It's the Soviet Embassy, look."

After the demonstration the day got steadily better. The

poets were surrounded by a group of Swedes, which was fortunate since Ervin had absolutely no desire to end up in that gang. Instead he was left in the care of the same old dears from yesterday. First they took him to McDonald's for a burger, then an elderly chap drove him around Stockholm and showed him the sights, and the plan was that some younger guys would take him under their wing for the evening. There was mention of sauna and beers.

How can you be happy being just an ordinary girl when under your nondescript exterior you feel, with every single cell of your body and in every single moment, the quivering call of the real world? What if since childhood you have never been drawn to the things which everyone else is drawn to, the things they all know the right names for? What if your senses are only touched by the really important things, those things which make you laugh that ringing laughter of yours just before they escape your grasp? Only a slight echo can be heard in response, in old verses, or a song with no words, led only by its melody. Maarja had a beautiful voice, beautiful and strong, but she preferred to sing alone, because she didn't like to be watched, and she never showed those old verses to anyone. It was impossible to talk about anything important with other people, with all those pointless, sensible people, who knew the current exchange rate for example, but couldn't understand why Pontu[2] was a perfectly good name for a teddy bear. She was not at all embarrassed by her pictures, each of them was just an experiment after all. She strove to capture the whole world in them, everything which passed before her eyes; she knew that then she would succeed in replacing the outer film which concealed the true light with a form that at least approximately represented it. So what if her creations were also far from perfect? And if they took so much time to produce? If only she could simply wipe away the detritus of everyday life which obscured the colours from view, just as if she were cleaning dust from a windowpane.

Maarja did not like having to walk quickly because she wanted to be able to forget that she had a destination to get to, to be fully aware of the space she inhabited at any given moment. So she had learned to allow plenty of leeway whenever she had to get somewhere by a certain time.

---

2   Translator's note: *Pontu* is a common name for dogs in Estonia.

Like today.

Because sometimes everyday things could force their way in. You could be lying in high grass and looking at the sky, but then they would come and bury you under a mound of earth, nail you shut inside a tiny box from which you would never escape, and you would be left to your eternal repose with the earthworms.

Then the only thing you could do is stand up tall. The sky won't disappear anywhere if you don't.

And this thing that she was about to do was her only way of not disappearing.

But that wasn't the sole reason. It gave her a buzz too, the same as the buzz she got jumping from a great height. Like at the youth camp in Poland last year. She and Helle had been hanging about chatting on the bridge there, and some guy had walked past and said that the river water was so cold that you would be crazy to go for a swim. And so without giving it any further thought they had both turned round, lifted their legs over the railing and jumped in, fully dressed and full of the joy which comes from being free to be themselves. There was so much laughter that evening as they dried their wet clothes by the stove, and their sandals still felt cold and damp against their feet the next morning.

That same buzz when you reach out your hand and you don't know if it will break you. But at least you know that you're alive.

Maarja liked walking in Kadriorg Park, popping into the museum, and then going to the Black Swan café for a cup of coffee and a teacake, which was superb there. The old dear at the museum ticket office let her in at the discount rate when she showed her art class student card, even if she wasn't really supposed to, and all the old grannies who sat and guarded the pictures knew her face by now.

And so today wasn't really very different to any other day … if it weren't for that little package containing three rolls of film inside the large handbag which she had bought on her trip to Poland – because you couldn't get ones like that in Estonia.

Oskar Meering's large statue of Kalevipoeg was in the far corner of one of the rooms. Maarja approached it warily. The idea of leaving a secret package in a museum seemed completely crazy, but when she got closer to the sculpture she found herself admitting that there might be some sense to the plan. Kalevipoeg was wading through the waves of Lake Peipus carrying planks of wood on his back, and there was a sizable cavity between the rough water surface and his knees, which would only be visible to someone bowing down right next to the sign with the sculptor's name on it, and only if they knew what they were looking for. Still. Maarja looked around. One of the grannies was sitting knitting a sock by the opposite wall, from where she could also see through the partition door and keep an eye on the neighbouring room. Kalevipoeg was actually outside her field of vision, and let's be honest, it would have been difficult to steal that hefty sculpture without anyone noticing. Was there an alarm system? Come off it.

But for Maarja it seemed like her every movement resounded through the empty room like the crack of a whip, or a vase smashing into little pieces.

She opened her handbag: snap.

She looked for the package of film: rustle, rustle.

She kneeled down and her knees announced: crack.

And then she dropped the packet of film into the hollow behind Kalevipoeg's knees, leaving the edge of it just visible. Plunk.

Alex entered Viru Hotel at the back of the group and immediately noticed a tense atmosphere in the foyer. A big coach with number plates from the Russian Novgorod region was parked by the door, and a large group of girls dressed in short leather skirts and fishnet stockings were being helped on board with their luggage. The tour guide, a man in his late twenties who had scant experience but knew how to make polite conversation, was trying to object, but two older gentlemen with moustaches didn't leave him much choice: the bus's destination was not going to be the Pirita cloisters, but the clinic for sexually transmitted diseases on Raba Street, where the whole busload was being sent for a week of treatment. The previous evening the entire group had descended on the hotel bars and restaurants looking for new male friends amongst the foreign guests, and for a while it seemed like they were going to be quite successful, but unfortunately one of them tried to pick up a KGB agent planted at the hotel, and by morning he'd compiled a list of the whole group and passed it on to his boss. Not out of concern for the hotel's reputation of course, but because he'd already recruited a dozen or so Tanyas and Svetas of his own as agents, and he got a fair amount of useful information from them; he also took a cut of the earnings from their main activities. He didn't want any competition.

I didn't make that story up, by the way.

Alex didn't bother trying to work out what the argument was about, assuming this was just the typical scene when a tour group departs. He was given a room on the seventeenth floor, and he glanced out of the window overlooking the town a few times. The decision of Lenbumprom's management – to organise the paper production in cooperation with the Estonian branch of the Soviet Forestry, Cellulose, Paper and Timber Ministry, rather than in the Leningrad region as originally planned – had at first seemed a little unwise, but now he was sure that it was perfectly sensible. He had a view of the old town which was out of this world, although even the most ordinary things, such as the sea, looked somehow different.

This was his first time in Estonia, and he already agreed with those who had told him it was a clean and orderly place with quite a high standard of living.

His final conversation with Tapani was still bothering him a little. The last time he'd been in Finland, Alex had called Tapani and thanked him for arranging the interview. He'd probably done so in the spirit of defiance, after the conversation with Vladimir Vladimirovich, to demonstrate, at least to himself, that he wasn't going to be pushed about by some fisheyed guy; and he'd been a little bit tipsy as well. He'd travelled to Helsinki with Svyatoslav Grigoryevich and the trip wasn't strictly speaking necessary, but Svyatoslav Grigoryevich's son was doing graduate studies at the Institute of Technology and desperately needed one of those new personal computers which were impossible to get hold of in the Soviet Union. That only became clear later, because when it was announced that Alex was going on a work trip, Konstantin Zakharovich and Olga Anatolyevna were terribly put out, both being higher up than Alex in the food chain. Svyatoslav Grigoryevich had evidently set things straight with them later, since they stopped making faces at Alex. Svyatoslav Grigoryevich promised to buy a bottle of Ballantine's for Konstantin Zaharovich, and for Olga Anatolyevna, Alex had to go to Stockmann supermarket's cosmetics department clutching a piece of graph paper with a brand of perfume written on it. That suited Alex fine since Tapani had invited him for coffee at a place just across the road, behind the Swedish theatre, and he had no reason to decline. But the perfume took a little longer than expected. Despite Svyatoslav Grigoryevich's assurances that the brand in question really did exist, Alex had to have a long discussion with the shop assistant about whether "Mazhi nar" meant *Imaginaire* or *Magie Noire*.

In the end they decided in favour of the latter, and Olga Anatolyevna later confirmed that this was the right choice. Alex was therefore a little late and stressed out when he got to his meeting with Tapani. Svyatoslav Grigoryevich had gone to a shop at Annankatu with a man from Karelia Trade to locate the right computer (he ended up with a very good model, a whole twenty megabytes of hard drive and two disk drives, as he later boasted), and they'd brought it back to the hotel on Kaisaniemenkatu by taxi. Alex had had to wait there to help lug two large boxes up to the third floor, which was after all the main reason why he'd been invited to come. Anyway, Tapani turned out to be very talkative, and told Alex lots of funny stories about the kinds of things which happened in joint ventures, and Alex had made a mental note of them so as not to bring shame to his country if similar things happened to him. But then he realised that he had to hurry back to the hotel, since he and his boss still had one meeting to go to, so he made his apologies to Tapani. Ahaa, of course, Tapani had said, gesturing to the waiter – but before you go I have a small favour to ask. Naturally Alex stayed seated. Tapani continued – they tell me that you are going to Estonia to do some business with one of the ministries, I've got an acquaintance in Estonia, would you be able to bring me a small package from him? Nothing too big, it should fit into your jacket pocket. It may be that I don't need your help at all, I'm asking just in case. You agree? That's great, someone will get in touch with you when you arrive.

> *When the big boss walks past,*
> *the wise peasant bows low*
> *and quietly farts.*
>
> *(Ethiopian proverb)*

At that moment Alex didn't have any problem agreeing to Tapani's request, particularly since he was in a great hurry. Fortunately he'd arrived back at the hotel room just a few moments before Svyatoslav Grigoryevich phoned from the ground floor. But now he was in Estonia, and after a short drive from the hotel to the ministry he was sitting at the far end of a long table, with a cup of weak coffee and a flaky biscuit with a dot of chocolate on top. By now he'd started to think that he may have agreed a little too hastily. Granted, no one had yet sought him out, but it did seem a little odd to be asked to deliver something from a complete stranger to someone else with whom he was only slightly acquainted. What if customs asked what it was? He didn't even know himself. On the other hand, he now had a bit more experience of going through customs, and he hadn't had any bother before. His blue official passport tended to have the desired effect on officials, especially if he was travelling as part of a delegation and his superiors were ahead of him in the queue. And anyway, Tapani seemed like a nice chap; surely there was no harm in doing a small favour for him.

They were sitting round the table, and a girl with dark bushy eyebrows handed out the folders containing the documents which explained what the Estonian side was proposing to contribute to the joint venture. When Alex arrived she leant down towards him and whispered into his ear: "There is a letter for you here as well," and then hurried off.

She didn't know for sure what was in the letter, but she was happy to carry out Uncle Valev's request.

Alex had problems keeping up with what was being discussed at the meeting, but he still managed to restrain himself from opening the letter until he was back in the hotel room.

Written on a slip of paper was the following message: "Tomorrow at Kadriorg Palace, 1400, Oskar Meering's Kalevipoeg statue."

Is it not entirely natural that having arrived in Estonia from Leningrad, a Leningrad Paper Industry worker – and withdrawn bachelor – should be more interested in the local art museum and Peter the Great's home than in Tallinn's main department store? Even if he is the only one? At least that is what Alex was thinking as he left the Viru Hotel after the group lunch and boarded the tram. They'd already checked out of their rooms but there was still three hours left before they had to be at the port. It was a sunny day and there were plenty of people walking in the park, but once he'd entered the palace and bought a ticket he discovered that he was almost the only person in the exhibition rooms.

But of course this wasn't exactly the Hermitage. The outskirts of Leningrad were as packed with palaces like this as an autumn forest is packed with mushrooms.

He carefully read the name tags of all the sculptures he could see, since he didn't have a clue who or what this Kalevipoeg might be. This became tiresome, since it was already several minutes past two and he was worried that the person who was supposed to pass him the package would give up waiting. But as he walked past the sock-knitting old granny and came to a standstill in the middle of the room he simultaneously realised two things: that the whopping great stone man in the corner of the room must be the Kalevipoeg he was looking for, and that no one was waiting for him there.

Why was that?

He walked up to the sculpture to make sure that this was indeed the right Kalevipoeg. Yes, there was the name Oskar Meering, 1890-1949. What next?

If he hadn't been so sharp-sighted then he might not have noticed the tiny package at all.

Hmm.

As I write these words my thoughts continually return to the same subject: the divide between two different worlds. For my children Soviet Estonia is like a distant planet. That's fine. I understand why, and it's better that way. Buying butter and vodka with rationing coupons is as far removed from today's everyday experience as the Second World War was for me during my childhood.

But those who do remember don't need much to bring that period back to life for them, together with all its sounds and smells, albeit fainter now. People who weren't there want more. And maybe they're disappointed when they don't see what they expect to see: pictures of Lenin the size of buildings, shops with empty shelves, and Soviet soldiers on the streets, smashing up the violin belonging to the little boy in glasses.

There were pictures like that, but we only saw them a couple of times a year, on the Communist public holidays. And neither were the shelves empty, it was more that no one wanted to buy any of the stuff which was available. It was true that you could only get hold of cars and other big items through work and waiting lists, or by paying twice as much (the "market price"), which the majority of people couldn't afford. But as far as I remember those wretched coupons were only around for a couple of years, when the regime was already on its last legs. As for smashed violins, you can see them in Soviet films, although they tended to depict the fascists doing the smashing.

Of course the Russian soldiers got up to all sorts of stuff here as well. And it wasn't just them. I recall one time when I was coming home on one of those dark winter nights after a school party – I must have been twelve or at least at the age when we had dancing at our parties – my hair was long, much to my father's consternation, and I was walking back carrying a plastic bag full of records. They were compilations of big band music performed by the James Last Orchestra and released by the Soviet Melodiya company's

Riga studio: my friends and I thought that the music was very cool, and those records weren't at all easy to get hold of. At that time there was a Russian-language maritime college next to our house, and the drunken would-be sailors often made a racket round the neighbourhood. They weren't really genuine "occupiers", like the soldiers, but they still wore naval uniforms. Anyway, on this occasion I was walking home down the empty street when one of them approached me and, without much ado, grabbed hold of my throat and pushed me up against the wall.

"Now then, let's see what you've got there."

"I haven't got any money on me," I replied, "please let me go."

"No, no. Let's see what you've got there," he said.

At that moment I truly believed that he wanted to take my records off me (maybe that says more about the particular historical period than anything else). But then, through his glazed expression came the dawning realisation that despite my long hair I wasn't actually a girl. And so he let me go and staggered onwards, while I went in the opposite direction, shaking.

To tell the truth, one can't say that this episode was unique to the Soviet Union. A drunken yob is a drunken yob whether or not he's wearing a foreign uniform. But back then I naturally held the Kremlin directly responsible for that brutish behaviour.

In the 1970s we took pride in believing that here in Estonia we were more cultured than in Russia, and we never normally had any reason to feel ashamed. In those days we were a cultural vanguard and not the backwater we are today. True, I know plenty of people who still feel disgusted when they see any kind of Soviet designs, because they are permeated with negative associations. And vice versa: on one of my first trips to Sweden, at roughly the same time as the events in this novel, I came across a shop selling fashionable clothes bearing perestroika slogans, amongst them was even a red cap with the letters "KGB" written on it in yellow. Evidently someone wanted such things.

There is no need to explain how different life would be in Estonia if we hadn't lived under the Soviet yoke for fifty years. Without the night-time knock-knock at the door. Tens of thousands of early deaths would have been avoided, countless homes would still exist, the Estonian nation would not have been scattered far and wide across the planet. But still, there are some things which would have been the same, or almost the same. True, in place of Soviet Sajaanid lemonade, we would have had Sprite. All of that time would not have been wasted in queues, money would have actually been worth something. And yet our parents and grandparents would still have yearned for light-coloured furniture in the 1960s and dark furniture in the 1970s, and miniskirts would still have come into fashion when they did. Equally I don't think it's right that our urban spaces are covered with garish advertising hoardings, just as our once virtually bare town centres would feel like some kind of aberration.

But our everyday life was different in some fundamental way back then.

What was different was a certain *feeling*. How we felt inside. Even those of us who were born decades after those night-time knocks on the door.

It's hard to explain if you weren't there.

"Now then, Comrade Captain, I've got one piece of good news and one piece of bad news," Vinkel said to Särg with a sneer. "And I'm guessing you want to hear the bad news first as usual."

"So you've found out where to get hold of bison shit then," Särg said gruffly.

"Right."

The two of them were standing by the window in the spot where the younger members of staff took their cigarette breaks, at the end of a corridor which was painted the repulsive shade typical of Soviet state institutions, although the paint was already flaking off. There was a glass jar full of cigarette butts on the windowsill, bits of white paper label still stuck to it where the glue had proved particularly stubborn.

Särg was waiting.

"I've got something on your son," Vinkel said hesitantly, almost reluctantly. "You really should keep a closer eye on him, to be honest."

Just in case you haven't heard this anecdote

The American Indian chief Winnetou was a character in the novels of Karl May (1842-1912), a popular German writer and a notorious trickster. A series of films based on these novels was shot in 1960s West Germany, with the lead role played by the French actor Pierre Brice, and the films proved extremely popular in the Soviet Union.

Anyway, the anecdote goes like this:

Winnetou gathers his tribe and says: "I've got one piece of good news and one piece of bad news. Which would you like to hear first?"

"The bad news, oh Winnetou."

"The bad news is that we've used up all our food, so we have to start eating bison shit."

> *The tribe grows despondent and starts to wail, then one of them asks what the good news is.*
> *"The good news is that I know a place where we can get hold of bison shit."*
> *Believe it or not, people found that joke pretty funny back in those days.*

You may not believe it, but the news came as a complete surprise to Särg. After all, he'd never had any reason to worry about Anton. He always got good marks at school. He'd finally started doing sport. He hadn't tried smoking, he didn't drink. He even declined champagne at New Year. It was true that he didn't particularly like talking about what he was up to, but he would always come home at the agreed time, and then just sit and read in his room.

"Really? Are you sure it might not be some mistake?"

Vinkel nodded.

"And what exactly is it related to?"

"It's that same case we've been dealing with." Vinkel tried to avoid sounding condescending, but the expression on Särg's face was so foolish. "Your Anton is consorting with our young insurrectionists."

"I find that very hard to believe!"

"So you think I'm lying then, do you? Eh?"

"No, that's not what I mean. It could just be a mistake, human error; maybe it's just someone with the same name?"

"We've got photographs," said Vinkel with a shrug. "I'm amazed that someone could be so blind to the truth."

As we know, Särg was actually pretty sharp-witted.

"I reckon I can guess the good news myself," he said.

"Right," said Vinkel with a smile.

"It goes without saying that I will do everything within my powers, Comrade Major," Särg assured him. First he just needed some time to think.

Alex met Tapani the following day. Tapani had called in the evening, as soon as Alex had arrived at the hotel from the port, when he had still been pretty worked up. What do I actually know about this man? Who exactly is he? On top of that a colleague had treated him to a toffee in the bar on the boat, which had caused a filling to come out of one of his upper teeth with a sudden crunch. That evening everything had been fine, but at night when he was asleep the tooth had suddenly started hurting so badly that it became unbearable. He had some tablets with him, which he always took with him because he knew that when toothache strikes you have to nip it in the bud. It wasn't like a headache, when you could just wait, hoping it might go away on its own. Fortunately he'd taken the tablets out of his bag and put them on his bedside table the previous evening. He got out of bed and took two tablets, but in his sleepy state it took him a while to find the bathroom door, and by then he was fully awake. He got back into bed, but he couldn't get back to sleep. The sounds of night-time Helsinki coming through the window certainly didn't help. What was going to happen? What if someone found out? I'm only twenty-six, damn it.

The following day Alex was free until two, and his toothache gave him a good excuse not to go trawling the shops at the Itäkeskus with the rest of the delegation. Tapani had invited him to a pizza place at one o'clock, and he had to eat something since all he'd managed to force down for breakfast was coffee and frankfurters; the scrambled eggs weren't nearly as nice at this hotel as the previous one, in fact they were downright disgusting.

His Finnish friend was already waiting for him at the restaurant, leafing through the menu with a jug of water and two glasses on the table in front of him.

"The *Capricciosas* are pretty good here," he said once Alex had sat down. "I ordered one for each of us, I hope that's OK."

Alex didn't care about that. He took the package containing the film from his pocket and pushed it across the table towards Tapani.

"Thanks," said Tapani, hurriedly shoving it into his pocket. "I hope it wasn't too much trouble."

Alex took a long look at him. Last night he'd spent some time working out how best to phrase the question which he now planned to ask. Such as, "Listen, are you messing me around?" Or, "Sorry, but I would appreciate knowing." Or, "We've known each other for a while now, perhaps you could explain who on earth you are."

But none of them turned out to be necessary.

"I can see that you're in need of a bit of clarity," Tapani said affably. "It's written on your face."

He took off his glasses and wiped them with a serviette.

"Look, I could of course tell you. But that would put you in a pretty tricky position. Because then you would need to choose. You could tell your superiors the whole story, but they would be surprised that you didn't come and tell them right away, even if you didn't tell them all the details. Or we could continue our friendship, although it would be a little bit different now. In that eventuality I would ask you to do what you have done for me just a couple more times."

As Alex tried to absorb the full meaning of those words, the pizzas arrived, placed on the table in front of them by a young man wearing an earring.

But so what?

"I would like to know what is on those films," Alex said.

"I should probably start a bit closer to the beginning," Tapani said, passing Alex a knife and fork. "We are both of the view that there are positive changes taking place in your homeland at the moment, is that not so? But we also know that many people don't like what's happening for obvious reasons. What we are doing is intended to help those who want to change your country for the better, make it more

113

humane, more open, a place where people don't have to live in constant fear."

"We don't live in constant fear," Alex interrupted him.

"Very well, very well," said Tapani, taking a swig of water. "Let's put it this way: we're trying to help those people who want to live their lives free from lies."

"But what is on those films then?" Alex asked again.

"They are photographs of documents, taken by certain very brave people." So things were pretty serious then, Alex thought to himself. "They are photos of the front pages of KGB agent files. I'm sure you will appreciate that it is extremely important for us to know who's who."

But Alex had actually been expecting something much worse. Now it turned out that they were only talking about some common snitches. He couldn't stand them, who could? But it was well known that the best defence was to make sure that you had nothing to hide. He knew that from experience.

"For example, it would be wise for you to bear in mind that a certain Mister Kalugin, Konstantin Zakharovich from your department is working for the secret services." Tapani pronounced the name with great difficulty. "So be careful what you say in his presence."

Really?

He certainly wouldn't have expected anything like that of that drunken lecher. Of course it was natural that there would be interest in their department; they were involved in joint ventures with foreign companies after all, but if he'd been taken on to work there, wouldn't he have been vetted already?

"How do you know that?" Alex asked.

"I just know."

Alex didn't have any reason to doubt him.

But taken altogether this could only mean one thing. That he was sitting and eating lunch with someone who was somehow linked to Western intelligence agencies. To those very organisations whose *raison d'être* was to force the Soviet Union to its knees and destroy it, as he'd been told for as long as he could remember. Up until now he had no reason to try to imagine what their agents might look like, so he was only capable of visualising them as those dogged assassins in long raincoats who chased Robert Redford in *Three Days of the Condor* (which he'd been to see twice). So what if Robert Redford was working for the CIA as well.

But he'd been told a great many other things too, and then told that everything was in fact the opposite to what he'd been told.

How can a person remain true to himself in such a situation? Tapani didn't seem too bothered by that dilemma himself.

"Supposing," began Alex slowly, "that I agree with you on this. I mean, that it's useful to know who is going to make complaints about their colleagues, and so on. You must surely understand that there's no way I would betray my country – that's all there is to it."

"You know what," Tapani replied, "I reckon that the ones who are betraying your country are the ones who want to keep your people permanently in the dark. It might sound high-flown, but that's how things are. I'm sure you know what I mean."

"You'll give me your word that there aren't any pictures of any, I don't know, airfields or port facilities on those films?"

"If my word actually means anything to you, then yes. You have my word."

Some things just are what they are

Alex and his mother had just come back from the beach. His uncle had left them the keys to his holiday home while he was away at a conference, and it was one of the few buildings in Olgino which was close to the sea, although it wasn't part of one of those state holiday factories. They'd walked along the wooden walkway leading inland with their towels slung over their shoulders, having decided not to get dressed on the beach as there were no changing booths nearby.

The black car was parked close to the front door, the men showed their official IDs, mother opened the door and let them in. Looking back on it now, Alex realised that the men had known that they weren't going to find anything. It was just their way of making a point. They chucked the plates out of the kitchen cupboard on to the floor, smashing them to bits, and they pulled the clothes from the wardrobe, ripping as many of them as possible. ("Please, they're my dresses!" – "Shut up, bitch"), but the books got the worst of it of course. There was nothing controversial amongst them, just Soviet editions of Akhmatova, Mandelstam, Blok. Uncle had bought them from the hard currency shops in Leningrad after his conferences, there was nowhere else one could get hold of them. They ripped the binding open, as if they suspected that the books contained messages other than those hidden between the lines of verse. Alex sat in his room, shaking. He was cold, still dressed only in his swimming trunks. One of the men looked in from the doorway, casting his gaze across the room with its empty walls, spartan bed, desk with no drawers, and the chair by the window, but he didn't enter. Their gazes met like a sword striking a shield. Alex and his mother returned to Leningrad that same evening, and neither of them has gone back to Olgino since.

Alex thought things over. On the one hand he was sufficiently naive to trust an intelligence agent, on the other hand, even if he did not realise it himself, Tapani was not actually an intelligence agent at all, he just had a lot of good Estonian friends in Sweden.

"But what if I get caught?"

Tapani sighed in relief, but Alex didn't notice.

"I can't promise it will be completely risk-free." He took his notebook from his pocket and looked for something inside it. "On the whole they don't search people like you at customs too often. But if it were to happen," he took a business card out from the notebook and handed it to Alex, "tell them that this person asked you to take the films to Finland to be developed because they don't process that type of colour film in Estonia."

Alex read the business card, which was in Russian. The name on it was Eduard Margusovich Põldmaa, of the Estonian Soviet Forest, Cellulose, Paper and Timber Ministry, department for foreign relations.

"He's a KGB man," Tapani continued. "He managed to harm quite a few people before they realised who he was. And it's quite possible that he could have got hold of those photos too, if he was working for the other side. So if you slip up, point the finger at him: it's only his word against yours, and they have more grounds to suspect him than you. If that happens then it will be the last time, I won't bother you any further."

It all sounded quite reasonable to Alex. If only his damned tooth hadn't started to play up again.

For a couple of weeks now Ervin had been living in a room which they'd found for him, in a building which resembled a dormitory and was about ten minutes' walk from Bergshamra metro station. He wasn't exactly overjoyed with the place. It was a pretty grim place – a bed, chair, table and cupboard, nothing else. On top of that he had to share the kitchen with darkies who often cooked their smelly food in the mornings. But he could put up with going to the kitchen once a day to heat up the oven-ready meals he bought from the supermarket, and otherwise he didn't have much need for it, since he had a kettle in his room.

On the whole he was disappointed with Stockholm. For the first few days it had been fun to walk round the old town and look into the shops on Drottninggatan, but all their prices were extortionate. There was no point in going into any of the bars. At first the journalists had shown an interest in him, and he even managed to cobble together some pocket money from the interviews, but they soon disappeared; after all he didn't have anything earth-shatteringly new to say any more. He could always drop by the Estonian House, and they would always be happy to see him, but there wasn't really much point. He was surprised how quickly he got used to the sight of the blue, black and white flag of Estonian independence flying there freely. But it was still a handsome sight, to be sure. He picked up the exile jargon pretty quickly, and found it easy to get talking to people. Lots of books which were banned back home were freely available in the library, but he'd always been more of a man of action, as he told the old grannies. And there was sod all to do there.

On one occasion he foolishly took one of the bottles of vodka he'd brought from Estonia to a party, which caused everyone to liven up, and they poured it out into shot glasses, which made for a promising start to the evening. But unfortunately a start was all it was; once it was finished most of them had to make do with tea, while a few of them, including Ervin, drank that light Swedish beer which back in Estonia wouldn't have been deemed fit for watering plants.

Another thing: there was little to talk to girls about other than politics. One time he went for a walk round town with one of them and a fancy limousine drove past full of shrieking, scantily clad girls. They were strewing bits of paper on to the street with the word TABOO and a picture of a wineglass and a telephone number on them. When he asked his companion what they were, she blushed and explained that it was a club – a sex club. Sweden was a free country, and freedom had its price of course. Ervin realised it wasn't a good idea to pursue the subject any further. He wouldn't have ventured into a club like that on his own, and it was likely to cost a fair bit.

As luck would have it the Bergshamra metro stop was just outside the central ticket zone. So there wasn't much sense going into town if he didn't have anything worthwhile to do there.

There wasn't much on television either. Eventually Ervin gritted his teeth, bought himself some sports gear, and started going running in the park. Just for something to do.

That was where they got him.

At first Ervin couldn't remember where he'd seen that chubby man with a moustache, but then the realisation hit him: it was one of those damned vultures from the demonstration.

"Well hello there, fellow countryman," the man addressed him in perfect Estonian. "Slow down a bit, would you?"

"I've got nothing to say to you," Ervin replied, but he came to a standstill all the same.

"Come now," the Estonian said, smiling. "Us guys are all from the same system, after all."

"I'm not one of those…" Ervin tried to think of a suitably rude word, but the man reached his hand out towards him.

"My name is Vello," he said. "I'm your new liaison."

"Listen, I have no intention whatsoever of…"

"Shush, shush," Vello said insistently. "You have no idea how long it has taken us to get someone like you planted into the Estonian community here. So it would be a real shame if we had to tell them what kind of character you really are."

In Vello's favour it had to be said that he wasn't always watching what he was spending, unlike Ervin's new acquaintances. Quite the reverse, he was always happy to buy the drinks. They met roughly once a week just to chat about this and that. Ervin told Vello what was happening at the Estonian club, and Vello told him the news from back home. Maybe he just wants to talk to an ordinary person in Estonian, Ervin thought, since the things I'm telling him, all that stuff about those poorly old folk, can't possibly be of any interest to anyone. Vello wasn't much of a drinker himself, but he always bought the drinks for Ervin, and he always came to their meetings with half a litre of Stolichnaya for Ervin to take home. They would normally meet somewhere in the back of beyond, in some working men's pub or Chinese restaurant on the edge of town, but Vello would pay for Ervin's taxi, on top of the money he gave him for the information, which was normally a couple of hundred krona a go. Ervin would always travel home by bus or metro of course – he wasn't in a hurry to get anywhere, and he had a pretty decent Walkman and all of Def Leppard's albums on cassette. Anyway, now he had a reason to knock about the Estonian club.

Raim was sometimes a little late. Like today, when he came straight from Li's place. Their bodies were now perfectly in tune, and they made pure music whenever they met. When he had eventually looked at the clock, it was clear he wouldn't even have time for a wash before leaving. He wouldn't normally have minded carrying the scent of his woman around with him, but he was afraid that Maarja might suspect something.

Although it was none of her business of course. Let her be jealous if she wanted. Anyway, they were now bound by something which was in some ways much more important.

But it did sometimes seem that everything was a game for Maarja, which worried Raim a little.

"Oh, I take my picture album with me now," Maarja explained. "And this fishing stool. I thought that if some tourist group suddenly came into the room then I could sit down and start drawing the statue in my book, until they went away. Anyway, there's not normally many people there."

"You should still be careful," Raim said. It was true, she really had to be careful.

Snap.
Rustle, rustle.
Crack.
Plunk.

Hmm.

The first thing which Alex noticed was her fingers. They must surely have been created to play the violin. The tiny spoon which they were holding looked like a foreign body, a heavy, artificial object which had planted itself there by force, but it still had no choice but to succumb, and so it danced gracefully on the plate with the cake crumbs, like a kung fu master in a Hong Kong film. This time Alex had decided to come through the park and go to the café a few steps from the tram stop to have a cup of tea and something to eat – he would get nothing on the boat, so he planned to buy some pastries to take with him too. He had the vague feeling that he'd seen that girl somewhere else before – perhaps it had been right here? – but last time his nerves had been so frayed that he'd needed two brandies to calm himself down. The girl glanced in his direction and seemed to recognise him too, but Alex just ordered a bowl of potato salad and a meat pie and went to sit at the opposite end of the room by the window.

It was already late evening and Lidia Petrovna was still sitting in the archives, as she was recently wont to do. The task of sorting out the agent files had somehow fallen to her. There was a huge stack of them, and some of them were really dusty, but Lidia Petrovna was primarily interested in the ones which had been taken out recently. She was already quite adept at using the Minox EC, and when she positioned the two table lamps so that their beams intersected she had quite enough light to work by.

She looked at the time. Each film had fifty-six frames, she'd already filled two of them, and the third one should be full by the end of the day, but it probably wasn't a good idea to stay too late, questions might be asked. First she had to take each file out of its folder to get a better view of it, put it on the table, take the picture, then put the file back in the folder, and then put the folder into the correct stack. On to the table, snap, back in the stack. Table, snap, stack. But what was that sound?

Lidia Petrovna slid the Minox EC up her jacket sleeve and turned round. Someone had definitely opened the door from the corridor, but fortunately there were two rows of shelves between her and the exit.

It must have been that dolt from the sixth department. She felt the Minox EC burning inside her sleeve, as if it were made from molten metal.

"Ah, good evening, Comrade Captain. I'm still sorting through these old files here, under orders from Fyodor Kuzmich."

"Aha, yes, I was just walking past and I saw light coming through the gap in the door, I thought that Marfa Nikanorovna had left the lights on again."

Two lamps, to be precise. Särg kept a very close eye on that woman.

Everything was more or less right.

Apart from that face.

Which was very pretty.

Although that was not all.

But Särg had other things to worry about now. He knew that he had to talk to Anton, but he kept putting it off, and he didn't share his worries with Galina either. One time he even went into his son's room when he was out, to have a look around. He picked up the papers on the table and opened one of the drawers, unable to believe what he was doing.

That's what things had come to.

No one would say this was love, because love is deeper, loftier, more far-reaching. No one would even say that this was passion, because passion is crazy, passion does not stop to ask: it just tears into little pieces everything in its path. That was how it was the first time, before words took over. But it wasn't like that any more. Casual onlookers would say look, there goes a middle-aged woman with her toy boy, or, there's a young man sowing his oats. But can either of those assumptions truly describe any relationship? There is always more to it than that, even though there are different ways of seeing these things. I would say: two people fallen from grace, entangled with one another but never to become one.

Lidia could clearly remember when nothing was yet lost. So what if her husband the pilot had disappeared off to Moldova with a hairy-legged stewardess, eventually to father a baby Moldovan. Whenever she saw herself in the mirror she knew she could get anyone she wanted, as long as her soul truly yearned for him. That memory stayed with her, although she'd never yearned enough for anyone to keep him close for long. Of course she had her visitors, and if one were to have a proper look in her cupboards, then the odd shirt, pair of underpants or worn-out toothbrush would be sure to turn up. But what now? Back then the school director had told her she should wear more modest dresses when teaching children who were at that tricky age. Both of them knew very well that Lidia Petrovna would never have entertained any improper thoughts. But now things were different. Permanently so. It turned out that her soul had longed for something else. She had just wanted to be yearned for herself, even if she knew that there would be a price to pay.

Raim could clearly remember when his whole life was still ahead of him. When he was at school he'd gone to acting club and found he was pretty good at it. If he'd been born a decade or so earlier he would have been beckoned by a lucrative career playing the brutish SS officer in one of those countless Soviet war films with more or less identical plotlines. But since he could not be born until his parents had decided they did not want to live out their long conjugal life alone, that option was not viable, nor was the prospect of studying to become a solicitor or doctor – in other words, making a career for himself as his parents would have wished. There had been a fleeting moment when he weighed up going in the opposite direction – Komsomol, international youth camps, romantic evenings by the campfire and Czech girls with names like Libuše. But he wasn't ready to betray his ideals. And he didn't particularly care what his parents thought. What was he supposed to make of two people who had been so ready to make compromises for the sake of an easy life? Exactly.

Lidia Petrovna is sitting in the kitchen in her dressing gown, smoking. Over the years she'd developed the ability to see herself from one remove, to make an accurate and sometimes harsh appraisal of herself, although that never caused her to change her behaviour, it didn't help her avoid constantly stepping into the same traps. And now it had happened again: she found herself waiting for those visits with her flesh, but not with her soul. After that first crazy afternoon (she'd eventually put the flowers in the vase and cut the cake into slices), she took a long time getting herself ready for their next meeting. She carefully chose the clothes to wear, the snacks to serve, the background music. She knew that they would never go to the opera, or a concert, or for a walk in the park. That was all right. It wasn't the most important thing. But now, when she didn't even apply cream to her face, or perfume her body in the places where she longed to be kissed? She took a cold, sober look at herself and concluded that this was a woman who had let herself go. Eventually her flesh would grow soft too, and the routine would finish off anything that was left.

Raim leans against the door frame, looking at her and thinking: how did I ever manage without her?

"I have to go now," he says, because he really does have to.

"It's not a good idea for it to be the same person every time," Indrek had told Raim. "You really should spread the risk. You might have such a pro tailing you that you don't even notice."

Raim had just got the latest consignment of films from Li and was supposed to go and meet Maarja to pass them on.

That had been an hour ago. Now Indrek was pacing up and down in front of the Kosmos cinema. He'd already thought up a reason why he and Maarja should go and see the jointly produced Soviet-Polish film *Witch's Lair*, about a space expedition to establish contact with wild tribes on a planet where evolution had gone off course, and work out where the concrete roads and sharp tools had come from. Indrek had decided that the film was just right after reading in the periodical *Screen* that it tackled sensitive topical issues using the medium of science fiction and allegory. Besides it was much safer to hand over the package in a darkened cinema. The main thing was that Maarja wouldn't turn out to be some prude waiting for her prince. Then they could go to Aigar's place – he'd gone to the countryside and left his keys with Indrek. They could light some candles and listen to Carl Orff's *Carmina Burana*, and see how things went. Hopefully she's not having her period.

And there she was. Not alone, as Indrek had hoped, but with a friend, the one with the long plait of dark hair, who was standing to one side and waiting for her.

"Raim couldn't come," Indrek said, quickly glancing left and right before taking the films out of his jacket pocket.

"Ah," said Maarja, putting the films into her bag. "Pass on my best wishes then."

They looked straight at each other for a moment.

"Bye then," Indrek said sullenly before going into the Kosmos cinema. Even if nothing had come of his other plans, it was still worth going to see the film.

snaprustlerustlecrackplunk/hmm
snaprustlerustlecrackplunk/hmm
snaprustlerustlecrackplunk/hmm
snaprustlerustlecrackplunk/hmm
snaprustlerustlecrackplunk/hmm
snaprustlerustlecrackplunk/hmm

"Excuse me, do you mind if I sit here?" the young man asked in Russian.

Maarja looked up. He actually had no reason to ask, as there was no one else apart from a couple of middle-aged lovers sitting by the window there on the second floor of the Black Swan, and there were plenty of other places available. But Maarja remembered this young man well: one time he'd been coming up the stairs just as she was leaving, another time he'd walked past her at the tram stop, and one time, or maybe even twice, she'd seen him drinking a cup of coffee and maybe a brandy by the counter here.

She could remember his eyes.

Let's make it clear from the start, this wasn't any ordinary young man.

"Of course, please do," Maarja said.

"Sorry to disturb you, it's just that it seems like it's not the first time I've seen you here, so I thought…"

"Yes," said Maarja.

"I have to go now," said Alex, "but I hope that this won't be the last time."

"Yes," said Maarja.

"Let's meet again, either here or somewhere else."

"Yes," said Maarja.

Karl could still remember that strange feeling of emancipation which overcame him the first time he consciously did something in a way his mother wouldn't have wanted. He didn't love her any less, but needed to assert his right to make his own mistakes. And to take responsibility for the consequences, even if that was the less enjoyable part of it. He had old-fashioned values, and no desire to go with the times. He couldn't understand people who had no problem doing so; he'd never been able to resign himself to the idea that this is how things are and this is how they have to be. He would've liked to have been a character in a Chekhov play, to be able to suffer a wasted life with dignity and nobility. But unfortunately he'd been born in a time and place where there was nothing dignified or noble about a wasted life – although that wasn't in any way his fault of course.

He'd been horrified to read about how the Soviet authorities had driven the chemist Jüri Kukk to take his life in a hunger strike, and others who'd been martyred for the cause of Estonian independence. So he'd joined the opposition forces to try and stop things like that ever happening again. Not so that they would happen to him too. He knew that the situation could not last much longer as it was: in all probability he would be sent to Seewald psychiatric hospital and pumped full of drugs until the world around him turned into amorphous semolina. Until he no longer cared. But however things turned out, he would never get his own life back now. Just like after a car crash, when you wake up in a wheelchair, or like a blaze that destroys your home. Some things remain, some things persist, but nothing can be as it was before. He'd heard about someone being taken all the way to Moscow, for "examinations", as they put it. There, you didn't even dare to eat the food: you could hide tablets under your tongue and spit them out later in the toilet, but you couldn't protect yourself from what they put in your porridge.

Of course, there was one other option: dropping out of the game altogether. Sorry guys, I honestly thought I was stronger. But my nerves won't take it any more. They're watching me all the time, at least it feels that way. It makes no difference. When we get our free Estonia back we will remember these times and we'll laugh about it all. But right now I just can't go on. I played along for as long as I could, but now I've had enough. The security services probably already realised that themselves, otherwise they wouldn't have let me out.

And don't think about telling me any more.
    Well, that goes without saying.

I reckon that the other guys have already guessed it themselves. I'm not in good shape. I can't take it any more. I'm not up to the work; I never was. I just thought that if I didn't do it, then who else would? And yes, it was more honourable to bang my head against a brick wall than pretend that it wasn't there. That's just who I am. That's me. The days were still almost bearable, but at night it got worse. But I don't need to tell them anything. They can see for themselves. That officer, that damned stamp collector, Särg, he can already see it (I can't help thinking it's a strange coincidence that he has the same surname as Anton, even if he seems like a completely different kind of person). But it's a good thing I was resolute right from the start: don't know … never happened … no idea what you're talking about. Of course it's all clear in their heads, but that's not going to hold up in a court of law. It's just some tough guy talking, nothing more. If they had witnesses, then it would be a different story. Of course they could find that wino. But why bother with that? They had no problems inventing witnesses. Like, for example, some random mum at the playground who saw from a distance … although we obviously won't reveal that she is our agent, will we. But they won't go to court. That much is clear. The days when you could cover up that kind of thing are behind us. The press would smell a rat. They'd pick up on the story. *Eesti Ekspress*, not *Voice of the People* of course. No one reads that one any more anyway. The lads would take care of things, they've got the contacts. And the KGB knows that all too well. That's why they're still keeping me here. But for how much longer?

I can't take it any more.

I've got to think up some ruse. Let's suppose – and I'm not saying I'm going to do this – let's suppose that I agree to what they want, then I'll get out and I'll tell the lads right away. Although that won't be enough for Särg of course. He'll insist that I tell them everything I know. But I'll just tell them that I don't know anything. Who did I get that envelope from? Someone gave it to me at an agreed spot by the picket; I'd never seen the guy in my life before. How did he know who I was? I made a prearranged sign. How did I know where to take it? A card came in the post, that's the God's truth. Who talked me into it?

Someone who is already locked up. Or has left for the West, then they can't check up. Madisson, that's who.

That won't work, it happened too long ago, I'd have to work out how to explain what I've been doing in the meantime.

There must be something I can do. There always has been before.

Could it be seen as a form of rape – in the metaphorical sense? When finally, having been asked many times, Raimond's father hung up his son's school graduation photo on the wall – so what if it wasn't exactly where his wife thought it should be – and then interrupted her as she watched her favourite TV series to plant a lip-smacking kiss on her cheek. Or perhaps it wasn't. In any case, mother didn't think so, she just let it happen, just like nearly everything else which she let happen to her. Without really noticing, and certainly without objecting, just like on those rare occasions when she let Raimond's father put his hand up her nightie and spent a few minutes on top of her and inside her, breathing heavily. After all, marriage consists first and foremost of obligations, so when one half fulfils their side the other half must do so too. A decade or so later people started to say no, it doesn't have to be like that if you don't want it to be. But she didn't know what she wanted. And neither in fact did Raimond's father. They could both entertain the idea that things could be different, but those thoughts came from the shade, not the light. Of course if someone had asked either of them why they tolerated it, then neither of them would have been able to answer, since neither of them would have understood the question. Tolerate what? It's just life, isn't it? It's just what it is. Rape? Come off it.

So is it any wonder that when people asked the same question about something which was far more profound, far more serious, they only managed to scrape the surface.

Outside, the weather was untypically chilly, the sky was clouded over, and the wind was blowing. It looked like rain.

How can I explain that they should only be afraid of things which are seriously scary? Maarja thought. She had one fear of her own which was as unfounded as they often are, but all the more pernicious for that: it's evening, she's in bed, having managed to get into the ideal position for falling asleep, lying completely motionless, so that her conscious self starts to extinguish itself from her body, and she is no longer joined to her arms, legs, back, since they are resting so gently against the quilt that they have no reason to make her aware of them. And then suddenly fear impinges on her consciousness: what if she will never be able to move again, not ever; what if she ends up lying like that for good? Her consciousness and her body are now independent of each other, living their own lives, but what kind of life can this be if it doesn't move, her body that is? But I can, Maarja tells herself, I can move right away if I want to, it's just that I don't want to, I'm in the very best position right now. Eventually she does move, just to dispel the fear, even if she has known right from the very start that nothing is holding her fast, that she won't find such a good position again. Of course she'd heard about the illnesses which suddenly para-lyse the whole body, leaving you locked in, so that you have to go through the rest of your life with nothing more than your memories. You never know what the future holds.

Generally the meetings took place in Tallinn every other Tuesday, and in Helsinki on Thursdays, so the delegation would arrive on the train from Leningrad on Monday even-ing, travel by ferry to Helsinki on Wednesday, and arrive back in Leningrad by Friday evening, no point wasting the weekends after all. But this time it turned out that one of the important people from Karelia Trade, without whom it was impossible to progress, suddenly had to go to Ireland for a couple of days, so the meeting in Helsinki was moved to Friday. We're sorry about that, said the secretary of the Finnish work group, but to make up for it we've booked you rooms in the Seurahuone Hotel, where the bar is open until four in the morning; there are several nightclubs nearby, and some of our guys will be happy to join you to explore Helsinki on Friday night; naturally, you are our guests. Which was nice of them, since there was nothing else to do there.

If this had happened on one of the first occasions, then Alex would have been very worried about having to spend a whole twenty-four hours hanging about this side of the border with the suspicious films in his pocket. But by now he was used to it. What's more he was carrying Eduard Margusovich Põldmaa's business card in a safe place in between the pages of his notebook. By now he knew him to look at as well, and you couldn't tell he was a spook by his appearance. He looked more like the boisterous joker type, the life and soul of the party, and was certainly popular with the girls from Leningrad Paper Industries.

So now they had to stay in Tallinn a day longer, which meant that they had a free evening. The ministry booked them some tables at the Viru cabaret, but there weren't enough spaces for everyone and it was made pretty clear to Alex that he would have to entertain himself. He could think of nothing better.

He set off on the familiar route from Kadriorg Palace to the Black Swan, wondering if that same girl would be there this time. Or maybe this Wednesday was exceptional in every way, and she hadn't managed to get to the park to sit and doodle in her sketchbook. But no, there she was, sitting there looking as if she were waiting for him.

"Hello again."

He put his coffee and meringue down on the table without asking. He knew that he didn't need her permission any more.

"Are you expecting anyone?"

"You," the girl said with a laugh, but Alex couldn't work out whether she was joking or not.

And thus it transpired that on that fine July evening, there in the ruins of the Pirita Cloisters, the Finnish pensioners who were waddling about between the walls of the church building which was burnt down during the Livonian War were joined by two young people. What's more, these young people dared to clamber on to the unearthed cell walls, up on to the half-collapsed roofs, walk up the steps which were worn smooth, and sit on the as yet untouched grass mounds, which must have hidden all kinds of secrets.

Maarja had studied Tallinn's architectural history at art school, so she could show Alex the rooms where the monks and nuns had lived and where the line which separated them lay. And so they stood either side of that line and imagined that there was an invisible wall between them, and that their outstretched fingers were touching the wall exactly opposite each other. They looked into each other's eyes as they did so, and naturally their fingers found the right place at the first attempt, and they held that position for a long time, or to be more precise, for a length of time which was impossible to measure.

Will I spoil everything if I kiss her now, Alex thought. Will I spoil everything if I let him kiss me now, Maarja thought.

What will each lover think of the other, when the infatuation has faded?

They strolled towards the exit, hand in hand.

Alex and Maarja walked on in the direction of Merivälja, stopping to buy a few bottles of beer from the pink shop on the corner, and then headed for the beach. It was a midweek evening so there weren't many people left there now, only one or two walking their dogs or just hanging about. The weather had been nothing to shout about, and although the sun was now shining again, it was still cool. Alex took his jacket off and laid it on the ground, and it was just big enough for both of them to sit on. He used one of the bottles of beer to lever the cap off the other, a feat which impressed Maarja. They spoke in a strange mixture of Russian and English, but Maarja knew them both equally badly, and so as she searched for the right words between sentences she would say, "er, you know" in Estonian, but they got by somehow. They knew each other better now: for instance, that in Alex's world, men always wore ties, while in Maarja's, people would only get up before midday if they had to catch a train or something similar. But when they looked up at the clouds stretched out across the horizon, they saw the same animals. There's a get-together in town tonight, you can come if you like, said Maarja. Sure, said Alex.

Ties and the system

One of my friends read the draft of this book and as well as making some helpful comments he asked why I often depicted people with Soviet sympathies wearing a tie but the freethinking Estonians without. As far as he could remember, it had been the other way round. Scholars who visited Tartu University from Moscow, for example, were surprised to see how formally dressed the Estonians were, while the Estonians, who considered themselves standard-bearers of pre-Soviet Estonian culture, were quite critical of their guests' scruffiness. Maybe it depends on which period we have in mind.

When I was at university in Leningrad you could spot a Komsomol activist by the fact that he didn't even take his tie off at the dormitory parties. I've personally had a fraught relationship with that item of clothing ever since middle school, where ties took over from red pioneer scarves as the system's favoured method of strangulation. Looking back, it could have been that a pro-Estonian education official introduced that requirement into the school system as a small act of defiance. But it was to inevitably take on the opposite meaning floating further up the sewage pipes of power.

And so there they were, sitting side by side on the floor in a smoky room on the second floor of a wooden house with a creaky staircase, where the toilet was outside on the landing. They were listening to one young man strum a guitar, while another played a small exotic-looking drum, and two girls sang, all of them sitting in almost complete darkness. Alex was the only one who could hear Maarja singing along, very quietly. They were holding hands tightly, getting a feel for where the boundaries lay between them, although they both knew that these boundaries were not fixed for good. Alex was confused, and this feeling had taken him unawares. Although he'd known Maarja for some time, he never dared to hope that they could be so close, and didn't know what to do next. She might be so free-spirited that she would be generous with her affections, but Alex was not sure if he wanted to be with the kind of girl who was generous with her affections (even if his body was telling him that he did). Maybe he would never experience another moment like this? The stars whizzed round at such incredible speed up above and might never be positioned exactly as they were today, right here and right now. But what would come next? Meat and two veg, a cup of tea, and TV? The blinding radiance would not last forever. A person has to know how to recognise the moment when it comes – to avoid living a life broken by regret. Bit by bit the darkness took Alex's world from around him, so that eventually only he was left, far from home, surrounded by forest, the sky and stars up above.

He must think that I'm one of those hippy girls, easy prey, already halfway to becoming just a pleasant memory, Maarja thought, although she somehow no longer fitted into her old self either. Then someone switched on a light in the corner, the musicians started to look a little tired, someone opened another bottle of wine. Tonya sat down at Alex's right-hand side and they spoke for a while in Russian. She was wearing a long dress, and when she sat down she hugged her knees and pulled them in towards her. Maarja knew that Tonya was prettier than her, that the red flush in her cheeks was completely real, that she knew how to talk to boys, it all just came naturally to her, and of course that splendid plait of hers was always on show. Alex told her about his work, the same things he'd told Maarja earlier in the day, but this time his performance somehow seemed more engaging, more inspired, and Tonya seemed better at showing an interest.

"I'm going to go now," Maarja said. "It's already late."

Without needing any prompting Alex got up too, poured Tonya another glass of wine, and then went out into the corridor with Maarja, where they found their coats in the big pile, and their shoes on the floor nearby. Outside, Alex took Maarja by the hand again. He felt her warmth against his palm.

Oh, if only she could live somewhere far from here, so that we would have a long way to walk together.

But it was not to be. In barely half an hour they were standing in front of a wooden house which looked similar to the one they had left, with a light on in one of the second-floor windows.

"That's my window," said Maarja. "Thank you, I had a nice day."

"Thank you too," said Alex.

"Do you know the way from here?" Maarja asked. "Or shall I go in and call you a taxi?"

"I know the way," Alex said, "and I know how to get back here as well."

It was not particularly hard to read the expression on Raim's mother's face when she cautiously poked her head round her son's bedroom door after giving a quick knock. But it was an expression which conveyed mixed feelings. She was bothered because someone had come to see her son, but curious as well, because the person who had come didn't exactly fit the image she had of her son's friends. And proud that this person, whoever he might be, had chosen to turn to her son when he was clearly in need of help. But let's take one thing at a time.

Raim never had guests come to visit. It had been that way for ages now, ever since the last time he had a group of friends round, which had been on his birthday, probably his sixteenth, and things had ended up getting a little out of hand. His parents had decided to leave the youngsters to themselves and had gone to the theatre, after which they had chosen to continue the evening at Mündi bar, where Raim's father was quite good friends with the doorman. They got home to find the corridor covered in vomit, and Raim wearing a slightly glazed expression. They fell out over that, because their boy was supposed to understand that even if no one could be reproached for moderate alcohol consumption, a wild booze-up like this was overstepping the mark. And a lot more had been drunk than those two bottles of Tokaji Szamorodni which Raim's father had bought them as a gesture of intergenerational solidarity. From then on Raim no longer celebrated his birthdays at home, which was a shame, since those parties had been good fun. Somewhere in one of the cupboards they still had a short eight-mill film which they had made of one of his birthdays, probably his fifth, but since they had no projector, they had never watched little Raimond blowing out the candles on his cake and looking up with a smile. Mother might have been surprised if she'd seen the film, since over the years some of her memories had been dressed up. It wasn't actually a good birthday for borrowing a camera because they had decided after a long discussion to give Raimond the doll which he so very much wanted, and of course you weren't supposed to give dolls to boys. And you definitely weren't supposed to record it on film – what would he feel if he were to see it one day? But that doesn't concern us now. He didn't have guests any more. And that was that. Did the man who had come round not know about that? He should have done, if he were one of Raimond's friends. He was probably a few years older than Raimond, true, with a pale complexion, true, and a shock of black hair, but he still seemed quite decent to Raim's mother, or at least he would have if it weren't for what had happened to him. He looked like he'd been beaten up, maybe even more than once, since the wound under his eyebrow had already healed up but he had a fairly recent-looking black eye. But then he didn't look like the kind of young man who loitered about town at night getting into fights: he was dressed too smartly. He was wearing what looked like a Hungarian overcoat – she'd wanted to buy one like that for Raimond, but they hadn't had a big enough size at the shop where her friend Ülle worked. Anyway, the young man's clothes weren't ripped or anything. A guest like that, without the bruises of course, would have been quite welcome to pop round any time. But it was still a little odd that he didn't seem to have anywhere else to go.

A few moments later Karl is sitting in Raim's room and they're trying hard to think up a reason why he has to stay there that night, since he simply can't be on his own right now. And why he looks like he does. They decide to say that some thugs broke into his flat, beat him up and tried to rob him. They smashed up the furniture, there was glass on the floor, but the main thing is that it's no longer safe to be there. Mother decides to believe them, although she realises that something isn't quite right, since some of his wounds are old ones. Be that as it may, she warms up some soup, then they all watch the TV programme *Think Again*;

that evening they make up a bed for Karl on the sofa – everyone gets into a scrape now and again, after all. And she's truly proud of her son – his friends must be able to see something special in him if they lean on him in times of trouble. Karl must be more seriously injured than even Raimond suspects, and he looks away as he answers their questions, suggesting that there must be something else amiss, but Raim's mother doesn't ask about that, because it's none of her business.

The following Monday Alex asked Svyatoslav Grigoryevich for three days' unpaid leave on personal grounds. By evening he was already on the train to Tallinn, and early the next morning he alighted at the Baltic Station. He hadn't slept very well because there were no places available in the sleeping compartments: all he managed to get was an upper sleeping berth in second class, and it was a little small for him. When he faced the wall he found it hard to breathe, but when he turned towards the corridor the light shone into his face. Of course he couldn't turn up at Maarja's door at eight in the morning, so he killed some time in a canteen which he came across on his way. He had a couple of warm onion pies washed down with meat broth, and after he asked nicely, the manager allowed him to brush his teeth in the back room.

He had no idea what was going to happen next. This was the first time he'd done anything like this.

But he couldn't wait longer than ten o'clock, and that turned out to be good timing, since he climbed the stairs and arrived on the second floor just as Maarja was coming out of her front door, carrying a small travel bag in one hand.

"Is that you?" she asked in amazement. "Here?"

"Yes, it's me," Alex said, suddenly feeling very foolish. Why had he thought that she would be expecting him? "Er, you know," he added, remembering the words he had once heard her say.

"It's certainly a surprise to see you," Maarja laughed. "Wait, I'll have a quick think. You know what? Come with me. I'm just off to see my grandma in Türi."

Alex had no idea where Türi was, but it went without saying that he was happy to go there.

It turned out that you had to take the train to get to Türi, which explained why Maarja was up at such an early hour. They sat opposite each other by the window, Alex facing the direction of travel, although he only had eyes for

Maarja. How could a girl be so impossibly beautiful, so pure to her very core?

As Maarja looked out of the window it seemed as if every building, every tree, every open view which passed by filled her with happiness. They chatted. Maarja's grandmother lived alone in a large house with a garden; almost everyone had a garden in Türi. And there was a lake there too. Maarja's grandmother had worked in a library until recently and now she was retired – but she had plenty of books of her own at home.

"And now she has enough time to read them all," said Maarja, summing up.

The train carriage was completely full, and it was no wonder, since it was a sweltering summer day and it looked like anyone who had half the chance was escaping town. An old lady wearing a headscarf and carrying a wicker basket sat down next to Alex, and her husband, dressed in a brown suit and a white cap, sat opposite. But it only became clear they were together when the man asked the conductor for tickets for both of them, since they didn't exchange a single word. A family sat across the aisle from them, and the little boy looked in their direction for a while until his mother told him that it wasn't polite to stare.

Maarja's grandmother was tiny, a whole head shorter than her granddaughter, but she had large eyes and a clear gaze, and she clearly took good care of herself and her home. Alex and Maarja had bought some meat and vegetables at the market by the station, since her grandmother didn't know that Alex, with his larger appetite, would be coming – although she anyway tended to make too much for Maarja alone. When she was introduced to Alex she replied in surprisingly good Russian, even if it did sound slightly reminiscent of Russian literary classics. The reason for her strange way of talking immediately became clear: when she was young she had the wife of an émigré White Army officer as her nanny. She'd once known French pretty well too, but there hadn't been much use for it in Siberia.

Later Alex and Maarja went for a short stroll around Türi: first they walked by the lake and in the church grounds, then they followed a sudden whim of Maarja's and got on a bus to go and see Laupa Manor. From a distance it looked like yesterday's cake, but it somehow didn't want to fit into the viewfinder of the tiny camera Alex had bought in Finland. Let's be honest, there was really only room for Maarja in his photographs anyway. They ended up being late for the bus back to Türi and had to hitch a lift. Alex found it a little strange that the driver didn't ask for any money, but Maarja assured him that that was how things were done in Estonia. Meanwhile, Grandmother had surpassed herself and the table was laden with a lavish banquet. After all, her granddaughter didn't come to visit very often, especially not in the company of a young man, even if he did happen to be Russian.

"I've made up two rooms for you upstairs as well," Grandma said, when all of them had eaten their fill. "Seems like a fine chap you've got there, although you could have tried to find yourself a decent Estonian lad."

"He's just a friend," Maarja laughed. "And I haven't known him for long at all."

How was she supposed to tell everyone? How could she explain to her dear grandma, her classmates, her playmates from the yard, that it was not light or dark hair, blue or brown eyes, nationality, citizenship, or even political views which made you a person, but the other way round. It was only when you were already a person that your hair, your eyes, your nationality and your convictions had any kind of meaning. But when Maarja looked at her grandmother again she realised that she didn't need to say anything. Grandmother was just carping as grandmothers always do. She understood everything very well. Without any need for explanations. Sometimes things were just what they were.

And it was true: Grandma knew very well that when something feels right there is no place for rational decisions, there never has been and never will be. That's just the way things are.

"Oh come off it," Grandma chided good-naturedly. "I've seen a thing or two in my time, you know." Then she switched to Russian. "I don't suppose the young man plays cards? In the old days visitors from Russia were pretty good at *préférence*, I don't know how things stand now?"

Alex had actually been a strong card player since his university days, although he hadn't had the opportunity to play for ages. Since they needed a third player, they had to explain the game to Maarja. It turned out that Grandmother's and Alex's understanding of the rules differed slightly, but that didn't matter, Maarja just laughed when they started arguing, and Alex could have listened to that laughter forever.

Alex couldn't sleep. Not because he was in a strange place: by now he was used to sleeping in a different bed every night. But he still couldn't quite explain the situation he was in to himself. Who were they, he and Maarja, and what kind of future did he want for them? There was certainly no doubt that he wanted there to be a future. And it seemed that Maarja did too. But what about this country, these people? It was as if they didn't really inhabit the same time and place as Alex did. Either that or he didn't belong here. Of course he had seen the occasional familiarly ugly building in Türi too, but they seemed like plants which had been put in the wrong flower beds, where they hadn't taken root properly. He didn't want to share the fate of those buildings. But he vaguely sensed that Maarja's laugh could purify him of everything which separated him from this place. Maarja's hands. Maarja's hair. Maarja's lips. Yes. Maarja's lips. He hadn't had feelings like this about either of those other girls he'd been all the way with. But this time he knew that he couldn't just behave like an animal, like a machine. He got up from the bed. What's happening, what am I doing? He pushed the door, it opened silently, he stood in the doorway, and at that very same moment another door across the corridor opened, and there in that doorway stood Maarja. What's happening, what am I doing, she thought. I hardly know this man, how can I be so sure that he is the one, the one I have been waiting for all these years? They took a few steps towards each other, and then Maarja's nightgown felt so strange to Alex's touch, less familiar than her skin. They said nothing at all to each other because they needed their mouths for kissing. Then they collapsed on to Maarja's bed and tore off everything which came between them, a little clumsily perhaps, but that didn't matter now. Alex was surprised and happy to discover that Maarja was not the type of girl who had been too generous with her affections: she had belonged to no one before, she had waited just for him. I am the only one who will be purified by that ringing laughter, Alex thought. Then he whispered the perfect sentence into her ear.

This page intentionally left blank

He spent the first waking moments in a state of shock. Me, her, here? He felt Maarja's hair gently tickle his chest; she was holding him tightly in her arms, as if he might otherwise disappear, evaporate into thin air. But that could not happen. Maarja was in his eyes, in his nostrils, in his flesh. Alex tried to remain motionless so as not to wake her, but she stirred, her hair brushed against his nose, and he sneezed.

Maarja opened her eyes.

The smell of pancakes was coming from downstairs.

The smile that should have promised summer

Years later Alex's fingers still chanced across that photo from time to time when he tidied his desk drawers; understandably he couldn't bring himself to throw it away. What went wrong? Had it been his fault? At first that question had so tormented Alex that he didn't know what to do. He could behold that image for hours on end, staring at the photo itself, or imagining it in his mind's eye. They had been rowing on the lake, Maarja was sitting in the boat, her arms outstretched either side for support, looking directly into the camera and smiling. The photo had been taken at slightly the wrong angle, towards the sunlight, and the little camera wasn't anyway the best. To tell the truth Alex wasn't the most expert of photographers either, but that wasn't the main problem. Maarja's smile was clear to see. Alex was in the picture too, at least his finger was, having let his finger wander into the field of the lens on the tiny camera. So at least they were still together in the photograph. But not anywhere else. Alex didn't know how to read that smile. It had promised an eternity. It had promised summer would never end. But things had turned out differently. So maybe he should have been able to make out something else in that smile as well,

> *something which foreshadowed loss. But for as long as he looked, he couldn't find it. Oh well, he'd been young then. His whole life had lain before him.*

Maarja had in fact come to help her grandmother pick blackcurrants, but when she tried to suggest adding that to the plans for the day, Grandma just mumbled something good-naturedly and told her to be on her way. Alex and Maarja went to the lake, even though neither of them had their swimming things with them, but it turned out that the boat hire was open. A man wearing a panama hat and a T-shirt with a picture of Donald Duck on it pushed their boat into the water for them. Alex grabbed hold of the oars and then they were off, away from the swimmers and sunbathers, towards the opposite bank, towards the island which they could see at the far end of the lake. Alex looked at Maarja and smiled. Maarja looked at him and smiled back. At that moment nothing could have been clearer for them. Certainly not the lake water – that was dark, with weeds of some sort growing in it which the oars got tangled in from time to time. And so here we were. If only it could last forever. Alex steered the boat around the lake so that not even the little town was visible any more, just the trees growing on the banks and the bulrushes, and the two of them. Just like in a film. He lifted the oars on to the boat so that he could rest for a while, and he looked at Maarja.

"You know, this is what happiness feels like," he said, but he couldn't help feeling that his voice sounded incredibly hollow.

The camera was hanging round his neck. Moments like this are impossible to capture on film, but still.

Then he realised that Maarja was singing. Not very loudly – someone standing on the bank wouldn't have heard. And it wasn't a song which Alex could have known, probably not even a real song with real words which could mean real things in some real language. It was Maarja's own song. Completely her own.

To this day he still feels lucky that he heard that once in his life.

Karl had kept putting off talking to the others. He still felt good when he was with them, and he didn't try to avoid their company, but neither did he seek it out. To tell the truth he didn't really think about things very much, he just went with the flow. He didn't know – how could he? – that his condition, or something very similar to it, had been medically defined, initially in a 1974 article written by Ann Wolbert Burgess and Lynda Lytle Holmstrom, in which they analysed the mental health of rape victims. It was the start of a whole new line of research in psychiatry. Anyone who is interested can find overviews of it in the specialist literature. It should be said that I am not in any way trying to compare Karl's experiences with real victims of abuse, especially since we are dealing with an invented character. But that in no way lessens the psychological trauma which these events caused him.

The other guys tried to look after Karl in every way possible. Indrek took him to the cinema to watch *The Dead Mountaineer's Hotel*. It turned out that Tarts had a decent stamp collection left over from the old days, and although he no longer had any interest in it himself he fished it out for Karl to peruse. But all this made it even harder for Karl to have the discussion which he needed to have with them. The security services had still not got in touch with him. He had a telephone number which he was supposed to call if he wanted to talk, although he didn't plan to ever use it. But his signature was there on the paperwork. He could never deny that. He'd used that to buy his way out of the cell which had stank of piss and sweat, which he'd been forced to share with one yob after another, although he was sometimes alone for several days in a row as well. That signature will always be with him, even after he explains everything to the others. Then they will know, of course. That he is not pure. That he is not like the rest of them. Not properly one of the gang. He could never be forgiven for that. But he certainly didn't want to be back in that cell, back before he'd signed that paperwork. In fact he didn't want anything at all any more.

In truth he hadn't actually betrayed anyone or anything. Of course he wouldn't have got out if he'd said nothing at all, let's make no bones about that, but then he hadn't said anything which the KGB did not already know.

In any case, Särg had believed that it would be enough. Or at least he pretended that he believed. It was a subtle game of course.

They were in the cellar. Karl had naturally come when he was invited; he had no reason to hide himself away.

"Ervin spoke on Radio Free Europe again yesterday," Indrek said happily. "Damn, he pulled off a blinder."

"Seems like that Ervin of ours has turned into something of a philosopher," Pille said with a clear note of irony, and nodded. "Next thing you know he'll be leading the troops into battle."

"And what of it?" Indrek said reproachfully. "He didn't say that the commies should be shoved into the gas chamber or anything like that, did he? He just said they should keep their distance, that there would be no place for them at the helm of an independent Estonia. Wasn't that how you understood it too?"

Pille shrugged her shoulders.

"Maybe that kind of stuff should be decided at the elections," she said.

"Now hold on a minute," said Indrek, refusing to back down. "At the moment the Supreme Soviet is pulling up the ladder behind it, passing all sorts of laws, making a dog's dinner of things, who knows how we're going to cope? If you want my view, I don't think that the Estonian Committee should be making so many compromises."

Karl found their constant bickering annoying.

"Where's Raim?" he asked.

"Oh, he's sure to be there at the teacher's place again," Indrek blurted.

"What teacher?"

"Lidia Gromova," Pille said. "The one who gets those photos from the KGB files for him, you know. She used to be the Russian teacher at our school." Pille and Raim had gone to the same school, although Pille had been there a good few years later, and only knew about Lidia Petrovna by hearsay.

"Then he gets to deliver the films to where they need to go himself, damn it," Indrek added. "We have to sit here like some wallflowers at a disco while other guys get to make history."

Maarja was waiting for him on the third floor of the Pegasus café. That was their special place, and neither of them would ever go there with anyone else. She was sitting at a table by the window, her large odd-looking bag on the chair opposite her.

"Greetings," said Raim, taking a seat and glancing absent-mindedly at her drawing.

It was a picture of a boat and a lake, with stars in the sky. And slightly to one side were four letters: ALEX.

"Who's this Alex then?" Raim asked in surprise. Maarja quickly crumpled up the picture.

"Oh, he's just a friend," she said. But she was actually glad to have someone to talk to. And so she told him about Alex, although not everything. About how they first met. And then the next time, before they properly got to know each other. How they went to Pirita. How Alex even came to visit her from Leningrad one time.

"Are you crazy?" Raim asked in amazement. "A Russian?" Of course he saw Li differently; her nationality wasn't relevant.

"What about it, I've got several Russian friends." Maarja said defensively. "There's Tonya at art school, for example."

"And he works in some joint venture?" Raim shook his head. "Are you sure that he's not a spook from some agency? They don't take any old person to work in those kinds of organisations you know."

"What do you mean agency?"

"You know very well yourself what we're up to, don't you?" Raim snapped. "And you're seriously trying to tell me that it was pure chance that this guy ended up being at Kadriorg at exactly the same time? Honestly, you're just like a little girl. He's obviously going there to watch that Finnish guy who comes to collect your packages. Why else would he always be there at exactly the same time?"

"But maybe he never goes into Kadriorg Palace? And those packages always reach their destination, don't they?"

"Yes, they do," Raim conceded. "Maybe he just hasn't got his hands on them yet. Or maybe they're just keeping the process under checks for now, how do I know?" But he'd suddenly become completely convinced that Alex couldn't mean anything good.

"I don't think so," Maarja said, turning bright red.

Maarja could feel the walls closing in on her oppressively, the ceiling getting lower and the floor growing cold; Raim carried on talking but it was as if he were speaking a foreign language. Her head was spinning, and it took all her strength just to keep her thoughts focused. Alex. Alex. Alex. But then what else can another person ever be to you besides a string of disparate memories, even if some of them have been imprinted on your skin, your version of those moments when you were together, plus the light and shade which your conscious mind – or maybe your senses – has added. These memories sometimes seemed to be explanations written by a third party, mixed with all kinds of questions about the real meaning hidden in his words and gestures. And what can you ever be to anyone else? As you know very well yourself, there are many layers, many nascent half-thoughts warring between themselves within you, but they are separated by a deep furrow from the outside world, and only some of them eventually make it out, over the bridge and out through the gate. Wasn't it reasonable to assume that other people experienced things the same way? Maarja was sure that this wasn't a question of lying, not necessarily. And it wasn't insincerity either. It was just part of being human: inside every person there is space for more than can ever be put into words or gestures, even if things do sometimes unwittingly slip out into the big world outside. And we're only talking about the things we notice, after all. I am not a tower constructed from iron girders, standing somewhere on a mountain top from where all is visible, but a hollow ship, which creaks

157

as it veers this way and that, only imagining that it knows where it is headed.

So how can I long for clarity, demand to really understand another person? Because that is truly what I want. I seem to be able to recall his physical form and the words he said, but maybe I don't, maybe I can only remember his voice saying certain things, sentences uttered in moments of greater certainty which I now remember so well – those moments are my medicine, my salvation, my fix. But even more than that I remember the line which joins those moments together within me. Can it be broken? It seems it can. It seems that these cold metal words can be inserted into me, like an endoscope. Words which I cannot digest, and which cannot sound in harmony with the orchestra of my being. The violins are awkwardly silent, the drums no longer thunder, the conductor has thrown his baton into the corner and is holding his head in his hands and yelling, but he can't be heard because those instruments were his voice. Now then. I have to pull myself together. I am an adult. What do I know? Only what I can remember. It's not a lot, but it is beautiful. Can there be another explanation for it? The honest answer is yes, there can. Does it change anything? Yes, it does. Does it change everything? Yes, it does.

They went their separate ways outside Pegasus. Maarja looked ill. Towards the end of their conversation Raim had to repeat nearly ever sentence several times, and even then he wasn't sure if Maarja had fully understood. Damn, she could end up under a tram or something if she wasn't careful. With the films in her handbag. But he definitely couldn't go with her. Instead he waved to her as she left, as if that would somehow protect her. But Maarja didn't look back once.

Whenever Raim was up to something which was even moderately risky he was sure to check whether he was being tailed. He'd done exactly that on his way to Pegasus. But not right now. That is why he did not notice how over on the other side of Harju Street, just slightly towards the Victory Square end, a woman came to a sudden stand-still. An attractive woman who was hurrying back towards Pagari Street after her lunch break, a woman who used to be a Russian teacher ... I probably don't need to continue.

No, I can't believe it, I just can't. That someone can look at me that way when he really has no other aim than to follow the tracks like a bloodhound, to find the hidden treasure. I just can't, and that's that.

"So, today is your last time here," the woman on the till said with a smile when Maarja greeted her.
"How do you know?" Maarja said in alarm.
"Next week they're going to start renovating the palace," the woman explained. "I've got no idea how long it is going to take."

Snap.
Rustle-rustle.
Crack.
Plunk.

Maarja had no appetite for teacake today. None whatso-ever. She walked out the gates of Kadriorg Palace and down the park path until she found a sufficiently large tree from behind which the museum entrance was visible. This can't be right. The next time we meet we'll laugh about it all. About how silly the world is, how silly people are. Or even better, we'll meet today. Maybe he is already in the café, coffee and meringue on the table in front of him, waiting and wondering where I have got to.
    She barely managed to wait ten minutes when a taxi arrived from the direction of town and came to a halt, and

then her very worst fears were confirmed. It was Alex who jumped out of the taxi and ran into the museum. A few minutes passed, and then he was out again. Off down the other path towards the café.

Now let's not fool ourselves. That could only mean one thing.

No rustle of trees to be heard, no crunch of gravel under the feet of the family walking past.

So that's that then.

How many pillows do you need to soak in tears before your eyes are able to see the world as it was?

How many letters do you have to rip to shreds before you realise that you never even knew his address?

How many times must the flowers bloom and whither before they can bloom for you again?

You have to have been there to know.

"I thought that I was your one and only," Lidia Petrovna said.

"But you are," said Raim in surprise.

"Oh really?"

But what do I actually know about this guy, other than that I am addicted to his body? Maybe he's got a whole coterie of women just waiting to come and drape themselves round his neck at the click of his fingers. That would be the most ordinary thing in the world for him.

"What's up?" Raim asked. "You're somehow … different today."

"Yes, that's right, I understand the world a bit better than before."

"Tell me what's the matter then." Li had never seemed so distant.

"All right. I saw you in town yesterday. You must have just been for a coffee. With someone else. But I understand of course, I'm only good for one thing. Well I do beg your pardon, I can't help being who I am."

"Ah." There was only one café Raim had been to the previous day. "If you mean that girl from Pegasus, then that's just a young artist I know." Raim was well aware that it was better for the links in the chain not to know too much about each other, but losing Li was a far greater risk. "She's the person to whom I pass the films you give me, nothing more. Her name is Maarja. We don't even properly know each other."

"Really?"

"Yes Li, really."

"My name's not Li, it's Lidia."

Raim said nothing in response, he just placed both hands on her head and ran his fingers through her hair, and her heavy thoughts melted away. Or even if they didn't completely disappear, they at least became insignificant enough for her body to be truly ready to receive everything which she longed for.

This time it was a bottle of pear liqueur, Xanté, which Vello produced from his briefcase.

"What's that?" Ervin asked in surprise. "You know I don't go for those poof's drinks." He'd been on familiar terms with his contact man for some time now.

"Of course I do," Vello said. "This is for you to give the hosts."

"Are the KGB about to put on a party or something? I wasn't aware that I'd been invited anywhere."

"That's not something you need to worry about," Vello said, and he started to explain.

The latest talking point in the Estonian diaspora community was the recent marriage of a young man by the name of Ahto. He'd been involved with the youth league of the Swedish Social Democrat Party for a while now, and had even visited Estonia once as part of their delegation, to meet the Popular Front and help make contacts. But now Ahto had found himself a wife from the Estonian homeland. And although this girl, who was called Tiiu, came from Käsmu just like Ahto's own parents, she already had a child by another man. Many of the Estonians in Stockholm doubted whether the marriage was a good idea, especially since quite a few of the local young ladies had their eye on Ahto. As a freedom fighter, Ervin also thought that it could be a major blunder. Tiiu herself might be fine and dandy, but hell knows who might turn up amongst her relatives, and there was nothing sensible known about the child's father either. He could have all sorts of dodgy acquaintances. And just think, this same child would start going to the Estonian School in Stockholm in a couple of years' time.

But others were of the view that everyone had the right to organise their affairs as they saw best. And that no one else had any business poking their noses in. These were free people living in a free country after all. Or were they not?

"Hang on, is that Tiiu linked to the security agencies as well?" Ervin asked. But Vello just scowled at him and carried on talking.

Apparently Tiiu really liked Swedish pear liqueur. And Ahto now had to demonstrate that he was a proper Estonian man, so it wouldn't be hard for Ervin the freedom fighter to get himself invited to their place if he got talking to Ahto at some event at the Estonian club.

"And then you should definitely go," said Vello. "And listen, when you get talking to them don't hold back with that talk about giving the Russkies a hiding: give them all the heroic swastika stories you've got."

"OK," said Ervin, although Vello's request seemed a little strange. "No problem."

"That's probably it for today then," said Vello, getting up.

"But you could at least tell me if that Tiiu is working for the security services," said Ervin. "I'll find out sooner or later anyway, when her file gets here."

"What do you mean?" Vello asked in alarm.

"Well, there have been films containing copies of the files delivered here from Estonia for some time now," said Ervin. "There's a special cupboard in the archive of the Estonian House where they keep the films and printouts, in alphabetical order. Don't tell me I haven't mentioned it before."

"Damned idiot!" Vello bellowed. "Damned useless piece of shit! Of course you haven't told me about it before, you damned shithead!"

"No need to be like that about it," Ervin said, getting offended. And he felt himself break out in a cold sweat.

He hadn't actually thought that much about it before. But now he realised that photographs of his own file could arrive any day.

Särg had never seen Vinkel in such a rage before.

"One of our own guys!" he yelled. "A damned rotten apple. Fuck, I'll give him a whack myself! I'll strangle him with my bare hands. I'll trample him into the dirt! I'll kick his head in, damn it! I'll fuck him up so badly that he'll be grateful when he's dead!"

"So what will we tell Kuzmich?" Ots asked.

"Nothing, to start with." Vinkel didn't want to think about what would happen when their boss found out. The whole damned network of spies! Heads would roll over something like this. The first thing to do was to work out exactly what had happened, and only then report to the seniors. The men nodded, they knew the score.

"Let's keep it to ourselves for now. Tell Vello to keep his mouth shut too," Vinkel added. "If that bastard realises that we know, we'll never get our hands on him."

"But then the leaks will continue," Särg said. That is if the person didn't already know. If it wasn't someone in that very room… Ots? Zhukov? They could just as well suspect Särg himself, especially Vinkel, or in fact anyone who knew about the Anton business.

"Let them continue, for now," Vinkel said with a sneer. "But now, Comrade Särg, your job is to put together a nice fat pile of agent files for them. Special editions, damn it. With lots of background history. The finest sons of the Estonian fatherland, as they say. Look about, read the papers. You could start with that damned Lennart Meri. Let them rip each others' throats out, the fucking scum."

"I'm sorry, but I just can't carry on doing it," Lidia said. She was holding the door ajar with one hand, dressed in her dressing gown and looking older than usual. She hadn't invited Raim in, and it didn't look like she planned to. "I keep thinking of how that dolt caught me; the next time I won't get off so easily."

After that time she'd felt feverish for several days, and

hadn't dared go close to the archive, even if she had a valid reason to do so – an obligation even. Raim eventually persuaded her to go back there. The camera was in her bag, but the first time she didn't even dare to take it out. In fact, she decided that she would give it back to Raim the next time he came for the films. Then she took a few pictures, with her hands shaking and her heart in her throat.

That's enough. All things have their limit. Let him sleep with those young Estonian girls; I'm not playing his game any more. That art chick of his, for example.

But now here he was at the door again with a twinkle in his eye, and clearly a little put out.

"The end is in sight, Li," Raim said. "Just a little bit longer."

She took a step back from the door and let him in. She might as well, things had already gone this far.

But there was something in the air.

Two things happened at almost exactly the same moment: Raim fell to his knees and took hold of Lidia Petrovna's waist with both hands, pressing his nose against her belly button, towards the spot where he longed to be. And Lidia Petrovna burst out crying, crying like she hadn't cried for years. Because once you start to cry like that, you cannot stop.

"It's nothing, dear," Lidia lied between sobs, and she stroked Raim's tousled hair, "it's nothing serious, really."

They got Karl just as he stepped out of his front door to go to work in the morning. Vinkel himself had sat in wait for him, in the car with Artyem whom he'd brought along mostly as brawn. They leapt out from either side of the car, Vinkel flashing his ID.

"I've got just one question for you," he said to Karl once they'd shoved him on to the back seat. "Who is it?"

"I don't know what you're talking about," Karl mumbled, his face turning completely white.

"Who is delivering information from the security services to your group?"

"Sorry, comrade, but…"

"That's enough," said Vinkel. "Don't play the fool with me. We know it must be one of our own. We know that you know who it is. We both know that you will tell us eventually anyway. So why waste each other's time?"

Karl sighed.

According to the official records he will die eight years later from alcohol-related liver disease.

In reality he was dead from that moment.

They decided to detain her in the act, so that no questions would be asked. Otherwise she might happen not to have the camera with her that day. Some guy called Karl told you? You must be joking? In any case, it would take some time longer to find out who she was passing the material to.

Lidia Petrovna had positioned two lamps on the table so that their beams intersected. She'd taken the first file from the stack, and looking back at her was a photo of a man who was getting on a bit, with a long face and thinning hair, and a big hearty smile. That face was familiar from somewhere. She took the camera out of her handbag, focused the lens and pressed the button.

And at that very moment Vinkel stepped out from behind the curtain.

I hope I never have to know how that felt.

"So this is what's going to happen," Vinkel told her. "First you're going to tell us everything you know. Then you will board a train. Have you heard of Oymyakon? It's in Yakutia. It breaks the record for the coldest place in the world every single year."

Särg was sitting in his office alone – for once the stool in front of him was empty. He pictured to himself how in an hour's time that very attractive woman would be sitting in front of him, having had some time in the cell to think things over. He didn't know why Gromova had done what she did, but there had to be some reason behind it. There always was. He wanted to know what it was. It would be easier for him to do what he had to do if he understood what had driven the person sitting the other side of the table.

But now another image appeared in his mind's eye, something which had given him no peace for the last few weeks. It was his son, sitting on the stool in front of him. Anton with two black eyes, and his eyebrow cut to bits.

We all have our reasons for doing what we do, Särg thought to himself. He has, and so do I.

Särg took his overcoat from the peg and left the building. It was lunchtime anyway. He walked down Pikk Street towards town – he had to find a proper telephone box, not just one of those phones fixed to the wall. The call he planned to make was not intended for passers-by to hear.

Galina answered almost immediately in her honey-sweet tones (come to think of it, why wasn't she at work?).

"Get Anton for me please," Särg said into the cold phone receiver.

"Hello Dad," Anton's voice came back at him a moment later, in Russian.

And then Särg said what he had to say so that later in life he would be able to look his son in the face, and at himself in the mirror:

"Lidia Gromova's been caught. In the worst case they'll know who she was working with by tomorrow, in the best case the day after. Tell your people. Right away."

"Wait, but how do you…" Anton started to ask.

"Later," Särg said, cutting him short, "you should go now."

"We can't," said Indrek, "We mustn't."

The other people sitting in the cellar were silent.

"It's a war," said Raim, holding firm. "There are always casualties. We've got more important things to do."

"Are you sure you're human?" Indrek demanded, quite angry by now. "Or some kind of fucked-up robot? Or have you decided to play God, damn it?"

"Hold on, don't get worked up."

Raim pulled away slightly. There was a sour smell coming from his friend's mouth, accompanied by globules of spit. Raim didn't think he was a robot. Far from it. But there was still a grain of truth in what Indrek had said. After all it had been him, Raim, who had picked up this girl and trained her to do something which could technically be classified as treason. In the eyes of the law the girl was therefore far guiltier than anyone from amongst their own ranks, which meant that if what Anton said was right, then she would find herself somewhere very cold for a good few years.

And what kind of leader was Raim if he couldn't look after his own people?

What's more he was also to blame. He had to go and mention Maarja round Li's that time.

"OK, I'll see what I can do," he said with a nod.

There were just the two of them sitting in the steamy sauna on Raua Street, but they were talking very quietly just in case. Valev heard Raim out in silence before going to douse his head in cold water. In the heat of the sauna his face was even more flushed than usual.

"I agree," Valev said once he'd sat back down next to Raim and splashed some water on to the sauna stones. "We have to try something. I've got this one idea, although it will take a couple of days, I'm afraid. The other option would be to send her to Lithuania, of course; there's all sorts of places to lie low there. What do you reckon, how long will Gromova hold out? How did she seem to you?"

"A little longer, I think," Raim said. In general he was trying to think about Li as little as possible.

"They're not going to show any mercy right now," Valev said apprehensively. "Very well then, let's leave the Lithuanian option in reserve for now. You can go there yourself if things really heat up here."

"I'm not going anywhere," Raim said resolutely. He couldn't explain to Valev why he was fairly sure that the security services would not know the exact details of his role in the whole business. But Maarja, that was a different matter altogether, unfortunately.

"Very well then, you know best," Valev continued. "We've got one guy in the ministry, and we can call Finland too. I hope that they don't muck around with the visa. Has she got a passport?"

"She should have. She visited Poland just recently."

"Very well. Go and find her and explain the situation."

On this occasion Tapani called Alex himself, which didn't happen very often, even though he knew the schedule for the Helsinki visits very well by now. Alex had only just got from the port to the hotel. He was still holding the room keys in his fingers and had just put his briefcase down when the phone started clanging. It was strange, almost as if Tapani had been waiting for him. Which made him uneasy. Especially since he didn't have anything to give him this time. Had he forgotten that?

But this time Tapani wasn't interested in any films.

"You will have to go back to Tallinn briefly tomorrow," he said.

"But what about the consultations?"

"You'll think of something. There's someone who needs to be brought over from there right away. She's got the paperwork to show that she's a designer in the joint venture; she's coming to Finland on a work assignment, let's say."

"Who is it?"

"I don't know exactly, a young woman. Just some person like you." Tapani seemed quite worked up. "When you get to Estonia someone will meet you and tell you where to find her, then you will whisk her straight on to the boat and back here. She's got all the necessary documents, but she doesn't know anything about the nature of the company's activities. So it's best that you accompany her, for safety's sake. I'll collect her from you tomorrow evening here in Helsinki."

"Actually I've got something I need to take care of myself in Tallinn as well," said Alex.

"Are you joking? There's no time."

"So this time it is going to be dangerous then," Alex concluded.

"Well, yes, I wouldn't say it's completely risk-free," Tapani admitted. "But if you get caught, you just play the fool, say that the Finns put you up to it, that you know nothing. She's the one who's got the most to be afraid of."

Back then everyone knew what it meant when they started broadcasting *Swan Lake* on the television non-stop – somewhere, something had gone seriously wrong, and even the Kremlin wasn't sure what would happen next. Like the day after Brezhnev's death, when no one knew who would succeed him. But this time the music sounded even more ominous, more unsettling than usual. Raim's father hadn't switched the television off once, and there on the screen Odette was gasping her final gasps for the nth time. They had long stopped actually watching it, but it was still on, just in case there was suddenly some new information. But the Kremlin had already said enough that morning. That's it. All over. A state of emergency had been declared. The military and security services were taking hold of the reins. While the little swans danced, the tanks were already rumbling down the motorway and could arrive any moment. Now there was definitely not going to be any hope of going abroad without official permission; in fact you'd be lucky if you ever managed to get out again. The best-case scenario might be a return to something like the Brezhnev era, Raim's father contemplated, but you couldn't rule out a new wave of deportations to Siberia and hell knows what else. Only time would tell. But at first there was no information at all. They tuned into Finnish TV now and again, but the only thing on was analysts making their assessments, trying to read the tea leaves but succeeding only in being annoying. Raim's father was standing in front of the drinks cabinet. To mark the sad occasion he'd decided to open the new bottle of Johnnie Walker, a gift from Jorma and Outi on their last visit from Karkkila that was supposed to remain untouched a few more months, until his sixtieth birthday. So be it, today was a special day. Raim was sitting on the sofa, feeling depressed, mother was in the kitchen, and there was ice in the fridge. Raim's father had known all too well that things would end up like this, and who was to blame? He'd always said that they shouldn't overplay their hand, and now look, they had this mess to deal with. But today he'd decided not to repeat this point. There was no sense rubbing salt in the wounds. His son knew the truth. And somehow they would find a way, they always had done. We Estonians have lived on this territory for six thousand years, and despite everything we are still here. Life wasn't just going to come to an end over this. Tomorrow is a new day, remember that. He'd even thought up something to say. A fine phrase for the moment when the whisky had been poured, mother came back from the kitchen with the ice, and the three of them were sitting on the sofa, raising their glasses, worried about what was to come and mourning what would be no more. Then he would say it: "To yesterday's dreams."

Maarja is standing in front of the mirror, looking at her reflection. She has almost learned the English text off by heart now: *Hello. My name is Maarja Pilv. I am an activist of the anti-Soviet underground. I need political asylum.* The main thing was not to start laughing, even if it did sound so silly.

By boat to Finland, on from there to Sweden – they don't check the passports on the boats in Helsinki. And then her new life would begin. It was high time now.

It's all a little like a dream. And it's best that way, since as soon as the real world impinges then the panic will return, the fear which extinguishes all will to live, which abides no other feelings. How else could she have expected to leave this place? But look, now you really can. It's simply that one life has come to an end, the life which promised all those things, all those things which nearly came.

So everything which is happening is for the best.

She messes up her words several times, but at least she can laugh at herself, more so today than ever before. Now she is allowed to. Who ever doubted that laughter can make the world a better place?

Hello. My name is Maarja Pilv. I am a simple girl. I believe in love. Whatever happens. I need nothing. No stupid Alex. Hello. My name is Maarja Pilv. I need nothing. Except love. Except life. A new life. Nothing political. Hello. My name is Maarja Pilv. Hello. Maarja Pilv needs a new life.

The sound of the news in Finnish is coming from the television in the other room.

"Mr Prime Minister," the journalist starts to ask, "you know the new president, Mr Yanaev, very well from your previous contacts. What kind of person would you say he is?"

"Given the current situation I would prefer not to comment on that," the prime minister says in response.

Out on the street there is silence too.

As a child Fyodor Kuzmich had never dreamed of becoming an astronaut, because no such thing had existed back then, but later in life he was presented with a real chance of becoming one. Once at the polytechnic institute he and two of his course mates were invited to a discussion on that very subject. By then Gagarin had already completed his mission, and conquering the cosmos had become the first thing since the taking of Berlin which the great Soviet homeland could take pride in. All those glory-seeking young men found it hard to think of much else.

But unlike his two course mates, one of whom did eventually get to orbit the earth, Fyodor Kuzmich was faced with a tough choice: space or mushrooms. Or to be more precise, the mushroom pies which Valentina made. In every other respect she was just like any other girl, but she was the only one in his world who knew how to make those mushroom pies which once tasted left you no way back. Especially if you happened to be someone like Fyodor Kuzmich, who had a special relationship with mushrooms. Back then he could sometimes disappear into the autumn forest for days on end, to return with bucketloads of beauties. He had no equal in hunting out the spawning grounds of the commonplace boletus mushroom, but he also knew how to find rarer specimens – the kinds which you would find no mention of in the handbooks yet Fyodor Kuzmich's grandmother would certainly have been familiar with. These mushrooms would then be duly transformed into incredible delicacies in Valentina's frying pan. This special relationship with mushrooms had survived to this day. He always took his holidays in autumn and spent them at his cottage in Laitse. His Ukrainian neighbour, a retired two-star captain who despite his advanced years still boasted a strong head of curly black hair, simply couldn't understand why Fyodor Kuzmich was constantly sloping off to the forest instead of enjoying the barbecues, vodka and good company at his place.

Mushrooms are older than humanity, he would say to himself, and somehow he felt that just recognising that fact could justify all manner of things in a person's life.

He didn't like living in Estonia. He wouldn't have had anything against watching a thriller which took place there, and he would tell his childhood friends from Volgograd that he liked the fact that everything was clean and orderly, but he knew he wasn't even kidding himself. He just couldn't understand the things he saw going on around him. He couldn't understand those houses or those streets or those people who walked down them. In fact it would be right to say that Fyodor Kuzmich understood Estonians about as well as Estonians understood mushrooms. Because if Estonians had the faintest idea about mushrooms then he wouldn't have been able to find such huge quantities in all their variety there in the forest near Laitse. In the same way that Estonians had a vague idea that some mushrooms could be tasty, even very tasty, while others were poisonous, so Fyodor Kuzmich believed that some Estonians were more or less loyal to the Soviet state, while the rest of them kept their fingers crossed for Finland when they played the Soviet Union at hockey, and did not accept the official reason for the Soviet Union invading Afghanistan. And who knew, there might even be ones like that amongst his own subordinates. Which made the situation even more complicated, since they certainly didn't dare say anything controversial to his face. But if they weren't working with the requisite belief and commitment, then clearly they were nothing more than scum. Anyway, he didn't know how to tell one from the other. For example, he would never have believed that the quiet nerd Särg was such a model communist that he was prepared to snoop on his own son. But nor could he believe that a model communist family was capable of producing a son who needed to be snooped on. Fyodor Kuzmich did not trust anyone whose behaviour was anything less than completely predictable. The years had taught him that things are not always as simple as they seem, and that it is often wiser to rely on a cynical careerist than an enthusiastic idealist, but that didn't essentially change anything. He could not countenance other people doing things which he did not approve of in his soul. By soul he of course did not mean the same thing that a priest might talk about in church, but something completely different … probably. But he preferred not to take that thought any further.

"Bring it on, Comrade Major," he said to Vinkel.

"Yes sir," said Vinkel, sitting down and putting the file on the table. "I can report that the enemy agent within our ranks has been identified and neutralised."

For some reason this did not provoke any reaction in Fyodor Kuzmich, which surprised Vinkel. Colonel Kuzmich even seemed strangely apathetic. Now that the KGB was picking up the reins of power he had every reason to be happy, didn't he? The military convoys were just about to arrive in Tallinn, after all.

"Well I never," said Fyodor Kuzmich eventually, as if reacting to something inconsequential. "Was it an Estonian?"

"Not at all, Comrade Colonel. It was Gromova, Lidia Petrovna, the typist."

For some reason that seemed to make Fyodor Kuzmich even sadder. So you couldn't even trust your own lot these days.

"Well, Hardi Augustovich, you're an intelligent person, you must know yourself that the game's up for us now," he said.

"Why's that, Comrade Colonel? This was just a one-off event, these days there is only good news coming from Moscow," Vinkel said in surprise. "At long last there will be an end to all this nonsense."

Fyodor Kuzmich shook his head.

"They're not up to the task. They're just digging their own graves, nothing more."

He had seen Yanaev's face and trembling hands on the television; that was no way for someone to look if he wanted to lead a successful coup. A rioting crowd is like a pack of dogs: if you show any sign of fear then the nearest mutt will have its teeth in your shins before you know it.

"I'm going back home to Russia," he said. "I'm sure they'll find something for me to do there. What about you?"

"Where is there for me to go?" Vinkel said, shrugging his shoulders.

"That's exactly it," Fyodor said, taking a bottle of brandy and two glasses from his cupboard. "That's what we've got to think about now."

Maarja liked the Harju coffee shop. They made really nice pastries there (I can vouch for that myself). And now this coffee shop was going to be the first stop in the journey which was just about to start, a journey which would be packed with pleasant surprises, and would go by the name of a new life. She had with her a small suitcase made from blue and red checked material with nothing too heavy inside it, just a few drawings and a couple of notebooks, her middle school graduation certificate just in case, one warm jumper, a toothbrush, and of course her teddy bear Pontu. Raim had told her not to take too much with her, just the most important things. She had her large handbag slung over her shoulder, with her passport containing the freshly issued Finnish visa nice and safe inside the zipped-up internal pocket.

All the bad things would be left behind.

She knew that she had to hurry, but she knew just as well that she would not be able to walk down this street again for some time, if ever again. So she wanted to take as much with her as possible: the grey arch of the doorway to her left; the typically high second floor windows with the sound of the piano coming through them; the famous fishmonger's a little way off, where the walls were adorned with those magnificent large paintings by Jüri Arrak – possibly the only fishmonger's in the world to be decorated that way. And of course the people as well: the old granny hobbling towards the shop with her net bag full of empty milk bottles; the young bearded father with lank hair and square-rimmed glasses, pushing a pram across the cobblestones towards her; a middle-aged man whose coat was clearly too long for the weather; two Russian girls standing on the corner examining a map of town. She preserved all of them in her mind, and they all became part of her. And part of her new life.

But that new life was in danger of ending even before it had begun.

It couldn't be. But yes it could.

Maarja glanced upwards for a moment. As if she wanted to make sure that the coast was clear.

But no, it was not.

There was a man sitting at the table by the window, an unforgettable man who was forgotten, or nearly forgotten by now: a Russian man, that special man. One of their men. Looking in the opposite direction, towards Old Market Street, as if he were waiting for someone. Maarja realised that it must be her that Alex was waiting for, that he was expecting her to come from the direction of her house, through the Baltic railway station, past the Schnelli Park ponds, then the puppet theatre and the Pearl coffee shop, across Town Hall Square, round the town hall building, from whichever side, so that eventually she would arrive at Old Market Street and appear from that direction, and he would spot her from a distance.

That could only mean one thing. Maarja turned pale and reached to the wall for support. They'd been betrayed, and now the situation was even worse than they feared.

"Excuse me, are you feeling unwell?" the old granny asked.

"Unwell?" the gloomy middle-aged man snapped back. "She's dead drunk, got no shame at all, in broad daylight as well!"

But Maarja saw something else: suddenly the old woman pulls a revolver from inside her coat and waves it at the two Russian girls, who throw the map on to the ground and adopt combat positions... The young father pulls a machine gun out of the blue pram... The gloomy middle-aged man sneers and pulls his coat wide open to reveal a mace... They are all ready, just waiting for Alex to raise his hand, and now he is already raising it, the signal will come any moment. By now Maarja has dropped her case and has started running as fast as she can back the way she came, certain that someone will shoot her in the back, or that another agent will emerge from the grey doorway and stick his leg out in front of her. The sky is purple, the people's faces are green, and the cobblestones are glinting orange with dots of coal black.

Another five minutes and I'll go, decided Alex, otherwise I will miss the boat. There could be all sorts of reasons why that woman didn't turn up; let's hope she hasn't been arrested.

Long, warm underwear, woollies, soap. Her toothbrush got left behind in her suitcase, and she doesn't have a spare.

They are in a heap on the bed and Maarja is sitting next to them, watching the door.

Because very soon someone wearing heavy boots is going to come through it.

She can't hear what's happening outside the room.

The hubbub which had suddenly ceased a couple of days earlier is slowly returning to the yard outside. A man in a vest has come out and is prising open the door of the shed. What does he want from there on this warm late-August day? We don't know. Helmi is hanging up the washing to dry. "Hey, Annika, have you heard?" someone yells out of the window. "About what?" comes the reply. Something about Yeltsin. There is music playing somewhere, someone must have guests round. Robert takes the rubbish out. "Hey, Robi, come and see what's up with this door," the man in the vest calls out. "The same thing that's always up with it," Robert says, going to investigate.

Maarja knows nothing about all that. She is watching the door of her room.

The pain in Raim's father's temples becomes unbearable at exactly the moment when the phone rings. Why does it always have to ring with the same intolerable bone-rattling jangle? And say what you like but whisky can give you one hell of a hangover. He and Raim drank a whole bottle of it yesterday, but he still couldn't understand what the appeal was. You were supposed to slowly savour it in some special way, not just down shots, which is generally the most sensible way to consume spirits. But they didn't keep any vodka in their house, that was more of a Russian thing, although they made an exception at weddings and funerals of course. Raim's father wasn't much of a drinker. Nor was Raim, judging by the look of him now, sitting there at the other end of the table, evidently in the same crapulent state as his father. It was good to talk to him, even if he didn't tend to share his problems much, which was understandable – he was a young guy after all. So that's it, then. It's all over. At that point Raim's father didn't know that at any moment his wife would appear at the dining room door and tell him to switch on the television. *Swan Lake* is over for now, there are people out on the streets in Moscow, Yeltsin is their leader, Pugo has shot himself, and here in Estonia the Supreme Soviet and Estonian committees are meeting on Toompea hill. All of this nonsense is over, over.

Maarja knows nothing about all that. She is watching the door of her room.

Fyodor Kuzmich was trying to keep his cool. He'd just finished a long phone call with Moscow, or to be precise, most of the talk came from the other end, he just listened and said, "Yes sir" now and again, but his television was on at the same time, and he was watching a direct broadcast of Yeltsin's speech. It was all very clear, even with the volume turned right down. He was experienced enough to draw the right conclusions – nothing which was happening surprised him. Vinkel was standing in the doorway watching television while Fyodor Kuzmich spoke on the telephone. Damn, now it's all going down the pan. Fyodor Kuzmich put the telephone down and beckoned him to come closer: they still had so much to do, and only a matter of a few hours in which to do it.

Maarja knows nothing about all that. She is watching the door of her room.

And me, what am I doing on that day? I step out of my front door and the people I pass on the street all have the same look in their eyes: they want to hug everyone they see. Although it does remain just a look – we are talking about Estonia, after all.

But it's a free Estonia now, that's true.

Ten Years Later

There's a young mother standing in front of the Konsum store on Narva Street. She has one child in a pram and another standing by her side, and her open coat reveals that a third is on its way. A man who is slightly over thirty, his face incongruously tanned, approaches from Viru Hotel at a brisk pace, and nearly walks straight past her.

"Oh," he says in English with a barely noticeable accent. "I almost didn't recognise you,"

The young mother looks at him in momentary amazement and then bursts out laughing, with that same ringing laughter which the years have done nothing to dull.

"Alex! It's you! Can it really be? What brings you here?"

"I'm at a conference," he says. "I live in England now, Oxford." He tells Maarja how he followed his aunt's advice and managed to get a place to do a doctorate at Oxford University, following which they kept him on to work in a research group dealing with transition economies. "And how are things going with you?"

"Quietly," Maarja says with a smile. "We've got our own company now: we import fluffy toys. I design the advertising. But I still paint now and then," she adds hurriedly, "or when I can, as you can see I don't have much time for that now..."

At that moment a fit young man with a healthy, ordinary kind of face comes out of the shop carrying two large bags, and quickly walks up to Maarja. No denying it, it would be hard to find a more decent Estonian lad.

"Let me introduce you," Maarja says, "this is Kristjan, my husband."

"Very nice to meet you," Alex says, reaching out his hand, "I'm Alex."

"An old friend," Maarja adds, just in case.

And now is probably the time to bid them farewell. As we walk away we just manage to hear Kristjan invite Alex to visit them at the summer cottage in Türi which Maarja's grandmother left her, and Alex promises he will, if he ever makes it back to Estonia. The wind carries their words away and whisks up the leaves from the ground, together with a few brightly coloured leaflets, as there happen to be elections on, and on that same pavement just behind Maarja and Alex there are two large banners, facing each other off. On one side is the Social Justice alliance, with Valev standing in the front row flanked by other members (let's put him there, why not?), on the other side is the right-of-centre Properity bloc, whose figurehead is unsurprisingly, Aare Murakas although there is a row of sensible-looking people standing behind him as well. Wait – it can't be ... can it ... surely our eyes must be deceiving us, no they're not ... yes, we really do know one of them from the old days. If we haven't realised yet, it's Murakas's trusted advisor and the bloc's candidate for interior minister, Hardi Vinkel.

But since you ask, I'll say one more thing: only a fool would throw away a beautiful apple from his own garden just because it has a few maggot holes in it. Only a fool prefers things which are shiny and never rot. After all, it's always the tastiest of apples that the maggots go for. And you can bet your life on it, the maggots'll know these things.

2009-2015